Totally Bound Publishing books by Sara Ohlin

Graciella
Handling the Rancher
Seducing the Dragonfly
Flirting with Forever

My Graciella
Hearts in Bloom
Harvest Moon Kisses
Winter Wonderland Love

Rescue Me
Salvaging Love
Igniting Love
Promising Love
Embracing Love

I0527721

My Graciella

WINTER WONDERLAND LOVE

SARA OHLIN

Winter Wonderland Love
ISBN # 978-1-80250-583-2
©Copyright Sara Ohlin 2023
Cover Art by Erin Dameron-Hill ©Copyright November 2023
Interior text design by Claire Siemaszkiewicz
Totally Bound Publishing

WINTER WONDERLAND LOVE

Dedication

To the lovely Marie in Cincinnati, a reader who reminds me why I write these stories — to connect and hopefully bring a bit of joy into the world.

Chapter One

Seeing her childhood home was more difficult than Poppy had anticipated. It was smaller than she remembered it, softer too, all covered in piles of snow. The front porch was bigger and much sturdier than it had been when she and her parents had lived there, when she'd thought the world was golden, when she'd thought they'd all been happy together.

She parked across the street so she wouldn't intrude and so she could get a good look at it. And she was glad she had because her gut clenched with the memories, and she shivered as ghosts skated over her heart.

An older man shoveled snow and a woman with curly white hair was sweeping off the porch. "Let's call it good and have tea, love," the woman said. "Getting dark soon and I don't want you to fall again."

"Yes, ma'am. Tea sounds good. What time are Jinny and the kids arriving?"

"Around six, their flight gets in." The voices trailed off as they went inside, closing the door and taking with them all the warmth. Poppy wrapped her sweater tighter around her and turned up the car's heat.

It wasn't her house anymore. It wasn't her father's either, apparently, despite her hope. *Maybe it hasn't been for a long time?* What had she been thinking, arriving in Graciella out of the blue and expecting everything to be the same, expecting her father to be there waiting for her? She hadn't heard from him in more than seventeen years. Out of desperation and loneliness she'd talked herself into this fool's errand.

Unfortunately, if he had been here all this time, then she'd have had to reconcile with the fact that he'd never once contacted her since she and her mother had left all those years ago. Honestly, exhausted, cold, completely drained, she wasn't sure which one she really hoped was true, now that she sat here facing her past and her present simultaneously with no way to understand the space between the two. Bone-deep weariness dragged at her soul as she headed out of town.

Poppy's pulse kicked up as she turned onto Brockman land. What caused the most recent surge of nerves was that she didn't recognize any of it. Of course, she'd never seen the farm's acres blanketed in white snow. Even the gorgeous apple trees, bare of leaves but donning inches of white powder, glistened in the fading daylight, like they were wearing diamonds and showing off, gone from barren rags to riches.

She remembered only one white winter when she was a child in Graciella, but playing in a small snow-covered backyard with her father was different from witnessing all these gently rolling acres hidden by soft powder. *Wow.* It even altered the main house. It had tripled in size, ballooned out with its winter gear on.

She parked beside several large pickup trucks and an old Jeep.

Had there always been that huge extension with all those glorious south-facing windows capturing the light? That was one memory engraved in her bones. Brockman Farms' main house had not been one of light, no matter how hard her Aunt Katie had tried to make it that way.

Now though, even covered in snow, perhaps because of it, the place had a magical and joyful embrace about it. Right out of a storybook. The house stood on the hill with the orchards stretching behind it. White Christmas lights graced the entire outline of the house. Flashing colored lights blinked in the pine trees to the side of the house and the shrubs along the front, and the biggest wreath Poppy had ever seen adorned the new double-doored entrance. *It's all so dreamy.*

Poppy pulled her aching, exhausted body from the car and nearly cried at the beautiful farm on the brink of early twilight, the sky and clouds white to match the ground, all the lights sparkling. Everything in this moment invited, *"Welcome. Come inside, child, and set down all your burdens. This is a place of dreams and warmth and happiness."*

And oh, how desperately she needed to believe it. She'd returned to Graciella to find answers to her most feared questions — why had her father abandoned her? And why did she feel, since she'd left Graciella, there was no place in the world she truly belonged?

Snowflakes began falling again as she made her way carefully to the front door in her old clogs, toes already stinging at how cold it was. Shoving her possessions into one suitcase and leaving her life in Paris to return to a place she didn't even know if she'd be welcome had been, what, a leap of faith? Or perhaps a lesson in disaster? From a quick search she'd discovered mean old TD Brockman was dead and Poppy's cousins ran the place now. She'd hurried and booked a last-minute flight to the US.

Now that she was here, would they welcome her, would they want to see her? *Only one way to find out. You've come this far, Pop, you can do it. You have absolutely nothing left to lose.* She climbed the front steps to ring the doorbell when laughter startled her. A woman and man headed in her direction from one of the paths that looked like it had been cleared of snow a while ago, only to have it start to become covered again. Huge, charming white flakes fell as lace upon the stone path.

"Hello," an enormously pregnant and smiling woman said. Her dark hair was covered in a bright green winter hat, curls trying to sneak out. "Can we help you?"

Poppy caught the woman's gaze and nearly fell off the step. "Liliana?" In all the years Poppy had spent following her three older cousins around, desperate to belong, Lily had been there too. She might as well have been family because she could always be found hanging around the Brockman brothers.

"Poppy?" the man said. "It's you! Dammit, little Poppy O'Brien! Where did you magically appear from?"

Those eyes could only belong to one cousin. "Turner," she whispered. Her favorite.

"Oh, my goodness," Lily squealed and wrapped Poppy in a hug. Before she could stop them, not that she wanted to, Turner's arms were around her too and they enveloped her in a massive smooshy embrace, Lily's baby belly begging for room. The best kind of hug ever and the kind she hadn't had in such a long, long time.

Turner opened the door, Lily linked her arm through Poppy's and rushed her through a gorgeously decorated hallway, yelling, "You guys are never going to believe who we found outside. Our very own snow fairy."

They rounded a corner into the old kitchen, which was also completely different from what Poppy remembered. But the aromas hitting her were all too familiar—baked dough, a hint of orange and spice. Other delectable savory scents hovered in the room. If a place could be the same based on smell, then this was the kitchen warmth of her childhood memories. And it was full of people.

"Guess who came home?" Lily said to everyone who'd suddenly gotten quiet.

"Pipsqueak?"

Cruz, her oldest cousin, sat by a woman with a sleek blue pixie bob framing pretty eyes. He was the cousin who'd teased her mercilessly, but who'd also taught her how to ride a bike. He'd always been the patient one, broody as he got older. Holding a sleeping baby over his shoulder, he stood and wrapped her in a side hug that was over way too soon.

"No way. Pop Pop!" Then it was Adam, had to be, the only one of the brothers who'd called her that as a child. They were close to the same age. As a boy, he'd been quiet and thoughtful and she'd been his Pop Pop. He set down the child he'd been holding, lifted Poppy off her feet and twirled her around.

"Jesus, when did you all grow into giants?" A laugh bubbled out of her. Her cheeks were wet with tears. They all smiled and talked at her at once. Adam turned her around and there *she* was.

"Aunt Katie. I..." The words stuck in her throat. She'd adored her aunt and hadn't seen her since she was ten. Once Poppy and her mom had left, they'd shut the door on this place for good. Poppy had so many unanswered questions. And ever since Poppy had left Graciella, she'd felt adrift. She wanted to anchor herself into this place she'd once loved and been loved in return. But now wasn't the time, with the kitchen full of more than family.

"Oh, Poppy, we've missed you." Katie's hug was fierce. "I'm so glad you've come. What a wonderful surprise. Sit and we'll introduce you to everyone."

Adam beckoned her into the banquette. "Poppy, this is my wife, Cass, and our daughter, Willow." He sat beside them. "We have twins too, but thank goodness they're at home with the babysitter."

Willow climbed onto his thighs and gazed at Poppy with large brown eyes, her hair a wild crown of curls. Poppy couldn't help but smile back at the little sprite.

"And Cruz's wife, Miranda."

The blue-haired woman gave her a warm smile and a wave.

They introduced her to their friends, to Katie's new husband, Javier, who gazed at her aunt with such deep love it made Poppy blush. They quietly showed her Cruz and Miranda's toddler, sleeping in the alcove. She got more hellos, and a mug of hot tea was set in front of her along with a plate. In the center of the table was a platter of cookies, another of salami and cheeses, little bowls full of olives, crackers and a tiny pot of honey, and suddenly her mouth was watering.

The last meal she'd eaten had been more than thirty hours ago, and one thing she'd never forgotten was what an amazing cook and baker her aunt was. "I don't know where to start," she said and gave a laugh. "But I'm starved, and the food looks delicious. Especially these."

"They are," Lily said. "Mini croissants with chocolate and orange. I dream about them. This baby is turning me into a pastry." Lily patted her stomach and took one of the steamy rolled pockets of dough, sighing with delight as she sampled it. She sat in Turner's lap, his arms tight around her. With a protective hand on her belly, he leaned in and nuzzled Lily's neck.

Poppy grinned. *Seems like he enjoys her pastry body just fine.*

"Where have you been all these years?" Adam asked.

"You're not the only one who left for a while," Cruz said.

"Nope. Cruz and Turner have only been back for a couple of years," Adam said. "Everyone comes home eventually."

Home. Adam sounded so certain. Poppy wasn't sure she knew the meaning of that word anymore.

The conversation continued around her. They plied her with food and more tea. Eventually someone passed around beer and wine. So much was happening, but Poppy didn't mind. She'd rather not ever have to explain what she'd been doing with her life.

"We made it!" A woman wrapped in a long winter coat trailed into the kitchen with more people following behind her.

"Yay! You're here," Cass said and nudged her way out of the booth to greet the new group.

"You sure picked a lovely time for a visit, Poppy. We're having a winter solstice wedding. Cass' friends Naomi and Bodhi from San Francisco," Katie said as she filled more wineglasses and checked the food in the ovens.

"Oh no," Adam said. "Where are we going to put Poppy? The big house, all the cottages, even our own houses are stuffed to the gills with people, at least for this week."

"What about Rafe's cottage?" Turner asked. "Or maybe it's not an ideal time with all he has going—"

"No," Adam said. "It's a good idea. I'll call him and check. We'll find room for you, Pop Pop."

Poppy hadn't even contemplated where she would stay, running from her current mess of a life to investigate her even messier past, on a whim...or such fierce loneliness. It was too difficult to make the distinction. And rock bottom hadn't led her to make the best decisions.

"No worries," Katie said. "Worries are for the morning. Tonight we're all going to enjoy a delicious meal together. Everyone grab a plate, fill up and find a spot to sit. Let's start this celebration week off right."

* * * *

"Okay, here we are," Turner said as he climbed out of the truck and helped Poppy unload her stuff. It was hours after she'd arrived. Now she was fed and deliriously exhausted. Poppy waved to Lily and climbed the steps. *Cottage? Seems enormous for a cottage.* But what did she know? Living in a three-hundred-square-foot attic apartment in Paris for the last two years had warped her perspective.

"Turner!" Lily yelled through her open window. "My water broke!"

"Holy hell," he swore and raced down the steps. He started to turn back, but Poppy waved him off laughing.

"Go, go! I'll be fine. Good luck!" Boy, she truly had picked an interesting week to visit Graciella. *"Everyone comes home,"* Adam had said. How she wished it was true for her too, that this wasn't merely a visit, but a return to the place where she'd felt the safest and happiest in her life. Before her family had been ripped apart and her trust in things like love and safety and family torn to shreds.

It had been dark when they'd all finished dinner an hour ago, but it was also winter and Poppy had no idea what time it was right now. She'd lost track on the flight from Paris. It didn't help that she'd arrived a day earlier than when she'd left. Her brain felt mushy, covered in layers of fog. The door was unlocked, which was lucky since Turner had raced away. Cruz had mentioned his friend Rafe leaving it open. That had been true when she'd lived in Graciella—most people never locked their doors. She'd love to get used to that type of living again. She dragged her suitcase inside, set the box containing her sewing machine beside an enormous, cozy-looking L-shaped couch and put the food Katie had packed for her in the refrigerator.

The place was clean and…spare, barren almost, if Poppy had a word. With only the sofa and a coffee table for furniture in the large open space, it felt nice at the same time, peaceful, with gorgeous wood floors. She was too tired to do much more than find a bed. The chill from earlier had woven its way back into her bones from her frozen toes. She needed to charge her phone. She needed to call her mother. A call she was putting off till forever, but a huge yawn and weary eyes urged her to find a place to sleep. A quick investigation showed two unfurnished bedrooms on the main floor.

Well, if there isn't a bed upstairs, I'll be fine on that couch.
She dragged her suitcase with her up the steep steps that felt like they went on forever and right as she got to the top, her worn-out suitcase decided to die an embarrassing death. The zipper exploded open and

sent all her belongings spewing out all over the hallway and stairs.

No! Poppy flopped down on the top step, completely shriveled up, exhausted. Even too tired to cry. She gathered her things, shoved them into the suitcase and dumped the old menace on the bedroom floor. Her tired eyes might be playing tricks on her, but if they were she didn't care, because before her was the softest, most inviting bed she'd ever seen.

Enormous and slick with a low headboard and so, so much room, with the thickest comforter calling her name. She dragged off her jeans and shirt and climbed under the covers. Aunt Katie was right—leave the worries till the morning. Suddenly she was warm and comfy and her eyes refused to stay open one second longer.

Chapter Two

The drive home from San Diego to Graciella had taken Rafe hours longer in the snow, and his stiff body ached as he finally climbed out of his truck in front of his house on the north edge of Brockman land. It was only a few acres from his friend Adam's house. The Brockmans had sold him the parcel for a great price, and he'd hoped to convince his mother to move here. He'd even built her a separate small cottage, so she could have her own space — a small one-bedroom with a large open kitchen-living area with windows on every side because he knew how much she loved the light. *Had loved*, once. Maybe her ghost would too. That was all he had left of her now.

He lugged his duffel bag out of the seat beside him, his limbs, his bones, even his muscles cramped from the fifteen-hour drive he'd made by himself. He was usually by himself, but it hit him now how truly alone he was in the world, with his mother gone.

He had the cottage, a workshop and now a house. Each one he'd built mostly with his own hands with help from the Brockmans, Lily's construction company and Javier. Even Katie had wielded a nail gun and a paintbrush a few times. The house and the small cottage behind it sat stoically under the black sky. Stars glinted off the snow. Quiet surrounded him. Peaceful was one way to look at it. Lonely was another. He had land and structures, but he was still one man all by himself. It was his life. *Best get some sleep and get on with work in the morning.*

He dumped his duffel bag in the laundry room, returned to his main living area and took in the space. Brand-new wood floors, brand-new kitchen, brand-new fireplace. He fell onto his brand-new couch. Yep, still the best purchase he'd made in a long time. Comfy enough to sleep on. He didn't own a television yet, but he didn't much care. Next on his list was finishing the stain on his bookcases.

Technically he had the next two weeks off, was supposed to be spending those with his mother. Now what would he do? Wouldn't take him two weeks to stain wood shelves. Ah well, his body relaxed into the comfort of the couch. He'd go to the barns, see if they needed help. They wouldn't mind. Which meant he better find his bed, because his neck wouldn't be thanking him in the morning if he fell asleep sitting upright on his couch.

Rafe didn't bother turning any lights as he climbed the stairs. The full moon lit his way, and his house was clean enough he could navigate blind if he had to. Plus, he registered slowly, the light was on upstairs. He'd barely managed to purchase a couch and a bed before the hospital had called about his mother. Not that he had many possessions anyway. He tripped on his way up. *Tired idiot.* He'd forgotten to take his boots off at the door. Oh well, that was one thing about owning his own home—he could keep it as messy or clean as he wanted. Not that he'd ever been a messy person. Why clutter things when it was easier and calmer for everything to have its rightful place? He should be happy he lived alone. That meant he could keep his house exactly how he liked it.

It took his fatigued brain several seconds to register the actual mess on his hallway floor or that his bedroom light was on, because he was trying to process the fact that there was a woman in his bed. She had his brand-new comforter burrito-wrapped tightly around her entire body, except for her bright red hair that curled around her head in a messy crown.

"What the hell?" he swore.

"Huh?" She startled awake. Shocked eyes rounded open, blinked, then she screamed like a banshee as she flung her body backward, landing with a thud on the floor on the opposite side of the bed and smacking her head on the wall. "Shit!"

"Hey." Rafe started toward her. Whoever she was, she'd have a bruise for sure.

"Don't hurt me!" she screamed.

He stopped immediately, raised his hands and started to back away, but he stumbled over something and fell into a suitcase sprawled open on his bedroom floor.

"Who the hell are you?" she yelled. "Go away."

"I l-li-live here," he gritted out. *Who the hell are you?* he should be saying.

"What?" she whispered.

She was a mummy, tangled tightly in the blankets. If he was tired from driving fifteen hours, what had she been through? Dark under-eye circles marred her pale cheeks full of fear. She had the look of someone who hadn't slept in years.

"Th-th-this is my house." He drew his arm around the room. *Why now?* Why in the hell were his words sticking now? *Because you're upset, Rafe. Calm down.* Except, hurt or not, a stranger had made herself at home in his bed. Her clothes were strewn in a mess all over his clean floors. And telling himself to calm never actually helped. Work helped. Fixing things helped. Tinkering helped. Not being around people helped. Not having to talk at all really fucking helped.

Her face softened, the fear mostly receding, as confusion wrinkled her brow. Neither emotion could disguise the washed-out exhaustion on her face. "Rafe?"

"Yeah."

"Oh my God, I'm so... I don't understand." She reached behind her to knead the back of her head. "I'm sorry. I thought... Adam said he called you to see if I could stay in your cottage. Then more people showed up at Aunt Katie's. I guess it's a party week...a wedding. Turner drove me here and Lily's water broke and I-I was so, so tired and my suitcase exploded all over. I left my life in Paris...ran away...came here to find out why...why my dad—And I can't call my mom because she'll be disappointed, so disappointed and oh..."

She wiped tears from her cheeks as they spilled over. "After *everything* that's happened, now I'm crying? What is wrong with me? I'm so embarrassed. Shit." And she covered her head with her hands.

What? Rafe tried to process her words. She was a stranger in his house, but she'd obviously had a hell of a journey. He eyed his bed and his own weariness hit him head-on, a wave barreling him under. He stood, peeled the deep green bra with black lace off his boot and quickly dropped it into the suitcase. He walked into the bathroom adjoining his bedroom, grabbed the tissues and, when he returned, held them carefully out to her.

"Thank you," she whispered. "What...uhm...what are we going to do?" Her eyes were wary and she gazed at him like he had the power to take her puppy away, if she had one. He wanted to pick her up and hug her, because she sure looked as though she needed one. *What the heck?* He didn't guess she'd be too comfortable with that.

"I'll sleep on the couch," he muttered. "Do you...do you need help?"

She quickly shook her head.

"We'll figure every...every...figure things out in the morning."

"Okay," she said.

He reached above her and snagged a blanket from the top shelf of his closet. Out of habit, he reached his hand to the light switch, but before he flipped it, she cried out.

"No! Please, I mean, can you leave it on? I-I don't like the dark these days."

Rafe sent a glance her way and even in those few seconds, the fear had returned to her face. "Uh, sure," he said. "The door locks...if-if you want." He pulled the door shut behind him as he walked out.

Faintly he heard her whisper, "Goodnight."

Rafe trudged downstairs. If he was dreaming, his subconscious was playing tricks on him, that was for sure. Removing his boots and his coat, he stood there, not knowing what to do. He'd better sleep in his clothes in case she wandered. *Don't want to make her any more uncomfortable.*

Rafe fell onto the couch and tugged the blanket over himself. He stared at the ceiling, suddenly wide awake with the image of scared but beautiful grass-green eyes and the scent of summer flowers teasing his brain.

Chapter Three

Light flooded into the room when Poppy woke. Beautiful windows next to the bed without any curtains or blinds announced that it was daytime. Poppy sat up and rubbed the dry ache out of her eyes. *I could sleep for a hundred more days in this bed. Glorious.* She flopped against the softest pillow ever. *Oh, shoot!* Last night came rushing back.

She pulled the covers around her and tried to put the pieces together. Adam must not have actually gotten in touch with his friend Rafe because Rafe certainly hadn't expected to find Poppy in his house, or his bed. *How embarrassing.* She'd have to find another place to stay because she couldn't steal a man's bed, not to mention the whole stranger aspect. She reached for her phone on the bedside table and remembered she hadn't bothered to charge it last night. What she did find, however, was a short, fat travel mug with a top on it and a sticky note underneath that said *Coffee.*

She pulled the top off. The liquid gold was still hot, and the smell pure nirvana. The taste was even better —

strong, dark, a hint of chocolate. She sighed. *I might be human again one day. Coffee and a shower.*

She stopped as she noticed her suitcase resting open against the wall. All her clothes and belongings were neatly folded and tucked inside. *Oh.* She blushed when she thought of the enormous man from last night touching her lingerie.

The shower and coffee had made a dent in her zombieness by the time she quietly walked downstairs. The place was empty. She took a moment to take it all in now that she had more brain power. *What a gorgeous kitchen.* Sleek black cabinets paired with cement counters. The kitchen opened to the living room with the couch she'd noticed from last night, where Rafe must have slept. An enormous granite fireplace graced one wall. Crisp white paint and wood beams lined the high ceilings.

Against the front of the house gleamed beautiful multi-paned windows and a long window seat where she could picture sitting for hours to read or nap, or maybe even draw again if...if her creativity ever returned. The other side of the front door had the same windows but with a corner bench built in and a small table and a precious nook with south-facing light warming the little spot.

No pictures or art hung anywhere. Nothing rested on the kitchen counters except a coffee pot. Even the open shelves sat bare. It all looked brand-new, clean and crisp and light. It also felt like something was missing and Poppy couldn't put a name to it.

She finished her coffee and washed her mug in the sink. The sink sat in front of two more gorgeous windows facing the backyard. Outside, Rafe used a shovel to clear a path between the house and a workshop-type building. Poppy grabbed her jacket, slipped on her clogs and was slammed in the face by a freezing, breathtaking day when she opened the door.

He'd cleared the steps and scattered salt along the path as he went. Thank goodness, because her clogs weren't made for this kind of weather. She shivered even though the sun beamed down on her. *Guess my jacket isn't made for winter either. But it's so pretty outside!*

"Good morning," she called, and he stopped shoveling to glance over his shoulder at her. *Whoa.* Poppy leaned back. Last night she'd been too freaked out then upset to really notice the specifics of this man. But the specifics said, *"Holy hell, he is gorgeous!"*

He towered above her, cast against the white landscape and bright blue sky. Demon or angel, an otherworldly combination of both. His black hair shone, thick and wavy. Almost charcoal, maybe brown eyes — she couldn't quite tell — stared at her and no hint of a smile graced his thick, luscious lips that parted slightly as if he were going to speak then decided it wasn't worth it. All she got was a nod in greeting before he continued his task.

"How did you sleep?"

"Fine," he answered.

"Thank you for the coffee."

A slight pause in his movement and another chin lift was her reward. *Hm, maybe he's still mad.* "I'm sorry about last night again," she said, and followed him as he shoveled. "I can find another place to stay. I appreciate you letting me have your bed. That was kind of you. It's a lovely bed."

Poppy hugged her light jacket closer to her body as the wind shot through her thin layers.

He paused mid-shovel, then moved his body back into motion. Strong arm muscles lifted a shovel full of snow as if it weighed nothing. He wasn't even wearing a jacket. Long gray T-shirt sleeves stretched along his arms and over his back...a powerful, beautiful back. "There isn't anywhere else."

"Oh." Her heart fell. *I really should have planned better.*

A pickup truck pulled up alongside the house and stopped in front of a smaller version of Rafe's house. It was to the side and tucked lovingly under a large tree. "What's that place?" she asked.

He paused again, his expression tight. "My cottage," he said.

Oh. That was where her cousins had meant for her to stay!

Katie and Javier jumped out of the truck. Poppy had liked Javier immediately last night. She'd never seen her aunt smile the way she did at Javier, a true and free smile, unhindered by the dark shadow of her first husband.

"Rafe." Katie went right in and gave him a hug. "I'm so, so sorry. What a difficult, difficult thing you had to do. But you're home now, where you belong."

Poppy followed all of this, curious. Something bad had happened to him, that much she could surmise. He seemed uncomfortable with the hug, or unused to it. That was a shame—his body was made for hugging. The thought heated her chilly body all the way to her toes.

Katie wrapped her up next. "Poppy, I'm so glad we caught you and that you've met Rafe."

"How are Lily and the baby?" Poppy asked, suddenly remembering the most exciting part of last night.

"Perfect and lovely and healthy. Theo, seven pounds, seven ounces. And the longest little toes I've ever seen. Can you believe it, her water breaking in the truck last night?"

"Better last night than tonight. Storm's coming. Good one this time," Javier said and took Katie's hand in his.

"We're off to the hospital, but I wanted to bring a few more supplies for you. But now that you're home, Rafe…" Katie rested her hand on Rafe's arm. "I trust you to help Poppy if she needs anything. We so appreciate you letting her stay in the cottage. She hasn't been home in years. She's important to us. But in case we're at the hospital for longer than we imagine, or the snow makes travel difficult tonight, I'll feel better knowing you're close by."

Javier took a few bags out of the truck and set them on the porch of the cottage.

"Rafe, maybe you could take Poppy to return her rental car?" he said when he was done. "That tiny thing will be useless in this weather and the snow and ice that are coming our way. There are plenty of trucks around the farm for you to use, Poppy, if you need a vehicle."

"That would be fine," she said. "But I don't want to impose on any —"

"I'll do it," Rafe interrupted her.

"Okaaay," she said.

"Grand. We've got to go. I didn't want you to think we'd forgotten either of you. The big house is open too if you need anything, and there are people all over the place doing wedding stuff. And, Poppy, I promise we'll catch up soon, lovely." Katie gave them each another hug. Javier shook Rafe's hand. They climbed into the truck and disappeared as quickly as they'd blown in.

"So, I accidentally ended up in your house, not your cottage."

"Yep." He stopped shoveling.

A man of many words. She couldn't help the feeling she was bothering him. Poppy followed him to the beautiful tiny porch where Javier had set the bags. Rafe opened the door and gestured her inside. Poppy brushed against him as she entered. The man was a furnace and she longed to arch into him. *Whoa, girl, settle.*

"It's finished, but empty, so-so it-it-it's good you-you found…my house last night."

"It's so lovely." Blond wood floors, a soft gray and white kitchen with pale pink marble countertops, another window seat and so many windows, even a skylight letting in the bright winter sunlight. His house was bright too, but this was more feminine. "It's beautiful, Rafe."

He swallowed, grabbed the bags of groceries and headed to his main house. She quickly shut the door and trailed after him. "I built it for my mother. It's empty, though—didn't have ti-time… Didn't get the furniture moved in. Doesn't matter now. You ca-can stay with me."

* * * *

Poppy. Rafe rolled her name around on his tongue, silently, of course. *If she's so important to them, why hasn't she been home in years?* Maybe she had one foot here and one foot in another land. A flighty wanderer, like his mother. The thought pricked at his heart, and he huffed off the feeling. He was sweating from the plowing and shoveling he'd done this morning, trying to stay busy while she'd slept in his bed. When he'd gone to check on her an hour ago, she'd been all bundled in the covers again, her face peaceful in sleep, showing none of the worry that lined her expression now.

"Are you sure? You don't seem too happy about…uhm, me." She followed him into his kitchen.

28

"I don't s-say things I don't mean." *Ever.* He barely said things at all. He washed his hands in his new sink. It was easier to talk to her if he wasn't caught in her serious gaze. Hard to do anything with those rosy lips of hers pouting right in front of him. *Or smiling.* Like when he'd been shoveling and looked over his shoulder at her. Her smile was brighter than the sunshine on snow, blinding his eyes and messing with his words.

She hovered in the doorway, perhaps unsure whether to really come inside or not. The tension reappeared in her face.

Why had he said she could stay with him? Then tossed out the fact that there was no place else. He didn't understand it. Only that the words had come out of his mouth. And he'd meant that, that he didn't say things he didn't mean.

He put the eggs and butter in the refrigerator, emptied the vegetables into his unused veggie drawers and lined the pantry with the rest of the groceries. Lastly, he set the loaf of chocolate chip banana bread on the counter and paused for a minute. It was his favorite. Probably Katie had known the cottage wasn't really where Poppy was staying. Probably thought pretty Poppy with the summer-green eyes would brighten his life. As if his life needed brightening. That was the last thing it needed. What he needed was for the holidays to be over so he could get back to work and resume normalcy.

"Hungry?" he asked.

A pause. She kicked off her shoes. Dumb shoes for winter, not high-heeled dumb like the sparkly gold ones he'd seen in her suitcase, but not meant for snow either. Course, they hadn't had this much snow here in forever. Weather patterns were changing. She should have boots and a better coat.

He drew his gaze up her frame. She buried her hands deep in her pockets and held herself tight, wary. When she walked around the island, it was like she was trying to take up as little space as possible. And he didn't want that. He didn't want to make her feel bad or uncomfortable, simply because he'd made himself that way by offering her a place to stay.

"Katie's banana bread, with chocolate chips. Still warm."

"That sounds good." She studied him. "Aren't you going to have any?" she asked when he set a slice on a plate for her and walked away.

"Already ate breakfast." His stomach was swirling all over the place. Just looking at her made him dizzy. Food would not be a good idea right now.

"My goodness, this is amazing!" Her voice was pretty when she spoke. Even nicer when she was happy. Her *my goodness* floated over him. "I remember Aunt Katie's baking. She was the best."

"Still is." Rafe had been here for almost four years now and he'd never, not once, seen Poppy. He'd have remembered. The way her green eyes and smile set fire to the entire room, the way she left a scent of flowers behind her, the pretty lilt of her voice that dug in under a man's bones and sang to him. Where had she been if she was family? Why had she not been around?

"Yeah. I'll, uh...finish and we can return my car if you want so then you can get on with your day. I promise not to bother you. But I appreciate you offering to drive me. And—"

"What's this?" he interrupted. He hadn't meant to interrupt. He knew it was rude, but sometimes his words spilled out whether he was prepared or not.

There were so many ways words could be awkward for him, which was why he preferred not talking altogether. It worked fine for him most of the time.

"Oh, it's my sewing machine." Poppy had come up beside him and the box that sat in his living room.

"You brought it on vacation with you?"

"Not vacation..." She shook her head and ran her fingers over the box. Long, graceful fingers, unpainted nails, silver rings on her index fingers. "It's important to me. It was expensive to check through baggage from France. I wasn't sure they were going to let me. There's no way I could leave it behind. I'm sorry if it's in the way. We can move it. Or maybe later, if you wouldn't mind, I could get it out and use it?"

Poppy ran her hands carefully over the taped-up box. She hadn't even had to say the words. From her reverent touch alone he would have understood that whatever was inside meant a lot to her.

Leave it behind. Her tone said she'd crossed the Iron Curtain and escaped with her life and a secret piece of wartime technology. *Hm.* He wondered what to make of that and tried to keep his mouth shut before he offered her protection from an imaginary monster. And why had protection leaped to the forefront of his mind?

She probably didn't need anything, especially not from him. People generally didn't need him for anything, unless it was for his engineering and water irrigation designs. That was fine. It was good to be needed for his brain and nothing else.

Chapter Four

"Graciella's bigger than I remembered," Poppy said, studying the new houses being built, visible as Rafe turned off the highway. The old streets of downtown came into view and Poppy smiled again at how lovely the snow made everything. "Or smaller too. Maybe because I'm not a child anymore." Silence greeted her as it had for most of the drive.

He was definitely a man of few words. And Poppy listened for each one. Sometimes it seemed difficult for him to talk, but other times his words were strong, certain. It definitely felt like he was mad that he had to talk to her at all. It shouldn't bother her because she'd intruded on him and there was nothing to say they *had* to know each other. But she couldn't stop watching him, taking notes on his serious eyes, how even though he didn't say much and often seemed mad or upset, his actions were polite. More than polite.

He'd not only let her stay the night in his bed but brought her coffee with a lid to keep it warm while she slept. Folded her clothes that she'd strewn all over his floor, offered to help her return her car even though every rigid muscle in his body screamed he wanted to be anywhere but here with her in his pickup. The truck was enormous, but the space felt small between them, tight. It was warm though, and she suspected he'd turned the heat up for her. *Thoughtful. He's a very thoughtful man.*

"Thank you for helping me."

"Mm."

They'd delivered her car to the airport car rental. It was good that he was driving them back to Graciella because the rolling hum of the ride coupled with the heat was lulling her to sleep.

When she thought they would continue toward the farm, Rafe pulled onto Main Street in the center of Graciella, and Poppy sat up straight. Her lulling comfort swooshed right out of the window. She'd only had eyes for her old house last night when she'd driven through. The whole town really did look different, and yet so much the same. Memories had a way of warping over time. Buildings had been renovated. The theater had morphed into a glittering spectacle, grand and open. A new bakery sat on the corner by the old post office. Snow gave the buildings a storybook air. Sidewalks had been cleared and holiday decorations sparkled.

And she could feel Rafe's eyes on her. He pulled his truck into a spot by a sports store with a retro façade that looked right out of the fifties. "Come on," he said. And there wasn't any discussion as he opened her door for her and held out a hand. She hesitated for a moment, not because she didn't want to take his hand but because she did. She did so, so much, and what even was that?

"Slippery," he said.

Poppy stared at him. He stared back. Maybe they didn't need many words between them, because it felt like even the air wanted to thread them together. As if he knew exactly what she was feeling and could feel it too, but didn't hide or hesitate. His eyes focused right on hers. They said, "Don't worry, I promise not to hurt you." She felt the moment everything shifted between them, a lock clicking into place. Without blinking, she slid her hand into his. *So warm and strong. I knew it would be.*

They both broke eye contact, startled or shocked. A spark zipped through her as soon as her skin made contact with his. He stared at their entwined hands. He must have felt her shiver as the bitter wind swirled around them, because he met her eyes again as he helped her down. And Rafe whoever-he-was didn't let go, but instead, tucked her in close to his side to shield her from the wind and led her into the shop called Woolies.

"You need a winter coat," he said. "Not sure how long you're staying in town. Boots too, probably. More snow coming." He let her hand go and rubbed his against his side. Hers still tingled.

Wow, with as few words as possible, he'd seriously confused her. He was worried about her being warm enough. The stress loosened in her belly as she studied him and took in his concern. But he was also annoyed at her. *"How long you're staying in town."* There was the tiniest edge of annoyance to those words. Or hurt. How could she hurt this man when she barely even knew him?

"Rafe. Good to see you." A tall, fit man with long hair and a gorgeous russet beard and mustache surrounding lush lips came from behind the counter to greet them. "How did your visit to your mom go?"

There was an uncomfortable silence and Poppy looked between the men. Whatever spark she and Rafe had shared outside that had set awe upon his face was gone now, replaced by a cold, lonely edge. "Short," he answered. And in a flash his face was back to granite.

Wait. Something had happened. Katie had mentioned it, and Poppy was still clueless. Without pausing, she moved in close to his side and squeezed his hand. He glanced at her. For one brief second, stark, open emotion etched itself across his expression. Grief or sadness — it was difficult for Poppy to tell.

"Sorry, Rafe. Hope everything's okay," the man said. "Hey there. I'm Johnny."

Keeping hold of Rafe's hand, Poppy gave the man her attention. He was gorgeous and he knew how to flirt with a smile and a glimmer in his eyes. "I'm Poppy. I just got here and I — "

"Let me guess," he interrupted. "You didn't expect this much snow and cold. Every year it gets worse. Although I love the snow. Makes it that much more fun to warm up afterward, eh?" He winked at her.

She laughed. "Wow. That's a whole lot of flirting." She waved her hand through the air.

"Too much?" He grinned.

"A tiny bit." She held up her thumb and forefinger.

"Well, I'd be remiss if I didn't aim it at such a pretty lady, now wouldn't I?"

"Oh my goodness. Now you're teasing me. And the fake Irish accent. That takes practice."

He laughed and gestured toward the women's section. "Who says I'm teasing ya?"

Poppy's laugh faded away when she peeked at Rafe. Whatever hint of openness he'd offered a moment ago was gone. His face had changed completely, sealed tight. He was as distant as if he'd been all the way in Paris himself.

"I'll…uh…" Poppy untangled their hands and stepped away from the force of it all and the confusion over how a near stranger could stare at her with such raw emotion one moment then pull the shade over his face faster than she could blink. "Go look for a coat."

There were so many beautiful winter coats to choose from. Short, long, a few with hoods. A rainbow of colors, even a shiny gold one with a hood lined with fake fur. It made Poppy smile, but it was a bit too flashy for her daily use. Her eyes kept getting drawn to a long sage-green one. Thick and puffy, it ran past her knees. The hood was edged with fur and the inside was lined with the softest cotton Poppy had ever laid her hands on. Wrapping it around herself felt even better. *I could sleep in this. I feel like a mummy, a cozy mummy.*

She closed her eyes and smiled. Warm and peaceful had been out of reach for her for the past few months. *I could sleep naked in this. Whoa!* Her eyes popped open, and she glanced in the mirror, hoping no one could read her thoughts. She gave a small giggle, because of course they couldn't. Rafe was on the opposite side of the store and Johnny was helping another customer. So she let her mind wander for a secret moment. Why would any woman show up with nothing on under a trench coat when they could arrive naked under this luxurious blanket of goodness?

"That one's nice." Rafe's voice out of nowhere made her jump and her cheeks warmed from her normal pale to pink in an instant. He had such a deep, beautiful voice, but not loud or needing the entire world to hear him. He stood next to the mirror and held out a pair of snow boots, gray with laces that went up the front. Inside they were lined with woolly warmth too. *I bet those feel wonderful.*

"Here." He stepped closer and studied her face with his dark eyes.

She swallowed the need to chatter away her nervousness. There was no way he could know what she'd been imagining. Only, his eyes had darkened, and she could have sworn she saw a flicker of desire flash when his gaze jumped from her lips to her eyes like he was drinking her in.

Oh wow. Her heart tripped over. There was the overt ridiculous flirting that Johnny practiced, then there was this quiet perusal. *Subtle but powerful.* That pulse flickered between them again. Trying to calm the shaking in her hands, she took the offered boots.

"Thank you, Rafe." *He has such a great name too. I want to say it constantly.* There it was again, the heat, and this time she could have sworn he almost gave her a smile. It didn't feel weird trying them on while he watched. Probably since he'd shuttered his expression again and crossed his arms in that cranky posture he was so darn good at.

Cranky, but handsome. *I don't think I've ever met someone who was cranky and cute at the same time.*

"They fit?"

"They're perfect." Poppy twirled in front of the mirror with her new coat and boots on, pleasantly heated from the plush material and from Rafe's presence. But when she stopped and turned around, he was gone again, heading away from her toward the front counter with her old shoes in his hands. Poppy gaped at him, too slow to understand he was putting all of it on his credit card.

"You really didn't need to do that." Wearing her lovely new coat and boots, Poppy followed Rafe out through the door. The tall, long-legged, frustrating man took large strides. He had a bag with mittens and a hat for her too, along with a separate bag with her old shoes. "I can pay you back, Rafe..."

He ignored her, sent her another cranky side-eye. Or maybe he didn't, and this was his way of answering, by not saying anything at all.

Rafe was swinging her bags into his truck when a door next to Woolies opened and the scents of garlic and tomato and spices hit Poppy so forcefully that she stumbled back a step. All thoughts of boots and money flew out of her mind. "Oh, my goddess. What in the world smells so divine?"

Chapter Five

Jesus, she was going to kill him. The way she held his hand, the sexy embarrassment on her face when she was trying on her coat. *Who wears a puffy winter coat and looks like they're having erotic dreams?* Those wide, soft eyes, the flush on her cheeks, her gorgeous mouth in that O shape, like she'd been caught doing something naughty.

He barely knew her, and he wanted to lie down in his bed with her, strip off every last layer and run his hands over what he knew would be the softest skin of any woman alive. He wanted to hold her head to him while he mapped a path across those lush red lips of hers. He wanted her on top of him, naked, while she explored his body and called his name in her sweet voice the way she'd done just now.

He was practically drooling with the fantasies. And it had to stop because it wasn't right. She belonged to the Brockmans, and they'd entrusted her to his care. Good thing he'd wiped his drool and stalked away from her. Good thing he'd paid for her new jacket and boots like a jealous boyfriend so Johnny wouldn't flirt with her anymore, and because he wanted to be responsible for her warmth. *Ridiculous.* He was losing his mind over a woman he'd met hours ago who was only visiting his world and would soon flutter home to the glamour of Paris.

And now she was moaning on the street over the heady aroma of Donny's Pizza.

It was good she didn't wait for him to answer because there wasn't even a chance of stuttering at the moment. His entire throat had closed up with desire. Confident now in her snow boots, she walked away from him, right into Donny's Pizza Pie.

Great, Donny. Another flirt in town. Did every man possess that secret art except for him? Rafe had a lot of thoughts right now. He'd thought Johnny was going to take Poppy's hand and kiss it in greeting, maybe sweep her off her feet with his A-game. When she'd laughed, Rafe's heart had stopped. Or maybe started.

It had hurt, whatever it was, hearing a sound so beautiful he thought it must have been a star shooting through the sky. His being had been altered at that moment. He might have said she broke him open, but it felt more like her beauty had sneaked inside his body, gathered all the broken pieces of him and started putting them back together.

And he'd thought he'd lost her before he'd even had her. Only, she'd kept holding Rafe's hand while she tossed Johnny's pass right back at him. But when she'd disconnected them, the thought running through his mind was, *she wants to run away.* It was a concept he was familiar with. Everyone important to him had slipped through his life on their way to somewhere else, somewhere better, somewhere more important. Or, in his mother's case, the past. A past that had hurt her every step of the way. A past she'd decided was more important than her own son.

He should get in his truck and leave. Leave Poppy there, be done with her. But that was the little boy inside him panicking. He'd had years to harden, to be strong in the face of disappointment. So he locked his truck, took a deep bracing breath of winter air and followed where the thumping organ in his chest urged him to go. He'd deal with the consequences later.

She'd brightened the entire restaurant by the time he stepped into the pizza joint beside her. Head tilted up, eyes closed, her smile was wide in awe. It was the most relaxed he'd seen her yet. He almost mimicked her and closed his eyes to feel what Poppy felt, pure bliss in her expression, but the hostess gave Rafe a wave and gestured to a booth by the front window. He tapped Poppy's shoulder to get her attention and led her in.

The place was buzzing with a healthy afternoon lunch crowd, families and friends squeezed into pale wooden booths. Donny's waitresses and waiters weaved paths with trays heavy with pizzas, ice-cold fountain sodas, beer and wine. Rafe drooled over the trays carrying baskets of hands-down the best garlic knots he'd ever tasted.

Eyes and mouth wide open now, she gazed around, lost in a delicious fantasy. A good meal could do that to a person. He'd never seen someone so open with longing for it. Or maybe he hadn't ever paid enough attention to another person—such acute, careful attention. A warning flashed in his brain, but he couldn't seem to help it. It was as though now that she was here in his life, on his path, his reason for being was to know her.

"Rafe, son. I heard you'd come in." Donny grabbed him in a hug before he could sit. Rafe hadn't been raised in a family that hugged — the gesture still felt odd to him. He wasn't sure how to react. "I'm so sorry about what happened in California."

Word traveled fast in this town. Rafe wouldn't be surprised if Katie had personally told each person she knew that Rafe's mom had died.

"Thanks, Don." Rafe untangled himself and slid into the booth across from Poppy, trying to ignore the way she studied him.

"You'll be okay. But anything you need, you ask. You hear me?"

Don had a way of offering comfort by issuing orders. That was his personality — gruff, but compassionate. A man could be more than one thing at a time — Rafe had learned that living and working for the Brockmans. *I'm not sure I'm capable of that, having many sides.* He was a hard worker, that was who he was. One-dimensional, calm, boring to be around, simple. He only needed to depend on himself.

"And you've brought someone with you." Don's gaze targeted Poppy and he frowned. "Dear Christ, Poppy O'Brien? Little Poppy? All grown up. You have the look of your father in you. His eyes."

"Uhm, hi," she said.

Her face was drawn again, similar to when they'd pulled into town earlier. Like a child who'd seen a boogeyman and wanted to flee as fast as she could.

Don must have seen the same thing, because he softened his demeanor, turning into the teddy bear he was with his wife and grandkids. "I knew your dad and mom, knew you when you lived here, when you were a little thing. Tragic, what happened. I'm sorry, love.

But I'm so happy to see you. How long are you here for?"

Rafe stared at Poppy. Her face was blanched white. Shock or confusion, for sure. "I'm not sure," she managed to answer. "A few weeks. I don't really...uhm...know my plans yet." Poppy flashed her eyes at Rafe.

"Poppy's been traveling. I th-th-think she's hungry."

"Right." Don swept his curious gaze between Poppy and Rafe. "Specials menu is on the board. Yell if you need anything." Don smacked the table and grinned. "Keep ahold of this one, Poppy." Don winked at her. "Rafe Holmes is the best guy you'll ever meet. It's a good day. Good to have you home, Poppy. You too, son." Then he was gone, strutting toward the kitchen.

"This isn't my home," she mumbled in a weary voice. She rubbed her hands over her eyes.

She was probably right. A home was where a person lived and breathed, where they started and could return to or made all on their own. She obviously hadn't been here in a long time and had appeared out of the blue. Besides, a home brought comfort and peace, and she was a horse ready to bolt, but one who was too beaten to do the bolting.

"Where is it then?" he asked. What the hell was he thinking? Conversation did not flow out of him normally.

She stared at him with eyes that were so much more than tired, he noticed now. They were full of doubt and anguish and loneliness. As if she'd traveled a million oceans to get here and lost everything she had along the way. *Does she always show every emotion on her face?*

"I don't..." She gazed out of the window. "I don't really know," she said softly.

And it sounded like the saddest song he'd ever heard. Her quiet didn't bother him. He preferred the quiet. But he sensed there was a whole well of noise inside her begging to come out and he wished he had the handbook for how to help her.

"Well, what, uhm, what do you like on your pizza?" He slowed his words and tried to relax his body, using the techniques his speech therapist had given him all those years ago. "Don makes a Graciella Favorite. Two kinds of salami, peppers, honey, basil and I don't know how many cheeses."

He was relieved to see her smile — tired and small, but it was there at least.

"An easier quest...question to answer," he said. But damn if her smile didn't short-circuit his brain, and all techniques he had for remaining cool sailed right out of the window. "You should eat. I think you're hungry."

I think you're hungry? Jesus, where did you lean to talk to a pretty woman? Exactly nowhere. At least not one he felt so uncomfortable around. So he sent out spurts of orders. *You should eat. What are you, a robot? Smooth, Rafe. Nice and smooth.* But dammit, his heart was racing with so many thoughts and feelings that he had a hard time untangling them, making sense of one over the other. And that was when he was always at his worst, talking-wise. But she didn't laugh at him, and the smile she gave him maybe even softened a bit more. Or maybe it was at the menu. *Hard to tell.* He was completely out of his league here.

"I'm starving. That pizza you mentioned sounds amazing. Want to share?"

He nodded. He wanted to share pizza with her. He wanted to share a whole lot more, and that scared the daylights out of him.

"What'll it be, you two?" Don's granddaughter Meg asked at the end of their table. The busy restaurant noise came back to him, the hustle of people, fountain drinks being poured, Don yelling orders to the kitchen staff. Busy and crowded though it was, Rafe loved this place. He always had. It felt like a piece of home to him.

"One large Graciella Favorite, two Cokes." She looked at him for confirmation and he nodded again. At Poppy, who was staring at him, wide-eyed, tired, vulnerable, lost.

"And…garlic knots," Rafe added. "Can't experience Don's for…for…for the first time and not have those."

"True," Meg said. She smiled at Poppy. "I guarantee you won't be disappointed."

Then it was just the two of them again, saying nothing. Even without words, something passed between them. Another part of being home meant making outsiders feel welcome. That was what he'd gone and done, despite the fact she was most likely another person in his life who would float right through on her way to anyplace more exciting.

Chapter Six

"That was the best pizza I've ever had. One of the best *meals* I've ever had," Poppy said. "You didn't have to pay for me, *again*. But thank you." Rafe had gotten the check when she'd been in the bathroom, then ushered her out and into the truck without a word. Actually, there hadn't been many words between them once the food had arrived.

She'd been hungry enough not to worry in the moment, but now she filled the silence with chatter because she was still confused. He'd been so nice, dragging her back from thoughts of her dad and her past into one fantastic pizza. And the garlic knots, heaven on earth! But now the harsh lines of his expression and the quick glare he aimed her way? Well, it was like he was mad at her. And she didn't know what she'd done. Or why it even mattered if he was mad at her.

One minute she'd feel a connection simmering between them, and the next he'd be ordering her to eat and insisting she was hungry. Which she had been, but she couldn't understand these many sides of him. And ordering garlic knots for her, then that scowl at himself for doing it? Really, Poppy had never been this consumed by another person's behavior toward her in her life.

Maybe she chattered because she was grateful, too. She'd expected to drive by her old house again on the way out of town and she hadn't been prepared to see it in the full bright daylight. To notice all the differences, to see that other family living in it. But he'd taken a different road, a new road that hadn't even existed when she'd lived here before. It was dumb really. She'd come to face the past, but she was too much of a coward to dig in and do it.

"Oh! Look at that," Poppy gasped.

Rafe pulled up to his house and let the car idle before he followed her and climbed out.

"Hi!" Poppy waved to her cousins. Adam and Cruz stretched out Christmas lights. Miranda was on the ladder under Rafe's roofline attaching the lights. Cassandra, Willow and Cruz and Miranda's son, Eli, played in the snow. Another couple wrapped lights around his porch railing. They'd strung garlands around Rafe's porch railing and an enormous willow wreath with a pretty bow now adorned his front door. Two enormous strollers sat on the front porch.

Rafe came to stand by her side. His expression changed from confusion to awe.

"Wanted to surprise you," Adam said. "Can't have a first Christmas in your brand-new house without any decorations. Especially this year. We decided you needed all the cheer we could bring."

"Rafe, good to see you, man." The man patted Rafe on the shoulder, then held his hand out to Poppy. "I'm Jake, and this is my girlfriend, Vivianna."

"Hello," Vivianna said. "So nice to meet you. We've heard all about you." She gently shook Poppy's hand then gave Rafe a quiet hug.

"Hi, Poppy!" Miranda waved from the ladder. "We came to check on you too. Didn't want you to feel left out with all the wedding events going on. I totally snooped at your box inside and saw the Paris airplane tags. I'm so jealous. You *have* to tell us everything about your adventures."

"Ahh, you've been in Paris. My home used to be near there," Vivianna said. She turned and smiled at Jake. "Now it's here."

Cassandra gave Rafe a hug too. "I'm so sorry about your mom. I know you hoped to bring her here to live. We'll take good care of you and probably drive you bonkers, but I know what it's like to hide with grief during the holidays, and it's no good. I promise we'll only annoy you a little. Then we'll let you have some alone time."

Poppy had already suspected something bad had happened to his mother. She hadn't let her mind travel all the way to the worst thing though — death. But the truth was right in front of her. She wanted to hug him freely, the way her cousins and aunt had done. *I bet he gives really good hugs. And I have pretty good ones myself to give in return.*

Part of her felt like it would feel natural to hug him and the other part wondered if he'd hug her back or do his statue impression and reject her. In that moment, with his unguarded expression, before he closed up again, she thought, *it doesn't matter what I need, this man needs comfort.*

"Rafe, carry me." Willow patted his leg.

She stretched her arms out and Rage obliged her. Poppy couldn't tell if he was uncomfortable or surprised. *Such a difficult man to read.* But Willow sure looked comfy in his arms.

The tiny girl patted his head. "Snowflakes in your hair."

Eli hugged his leg and giggled.

Poppy blinked at the picture. A snowflake caught on her eyelid. It was snowing again. Enormous flakes drifted silently around them. It was so beautiful that Poppy let her worries fade away. She closed her eyes, twirled under the snowflakes and breathed in the stunning scent of a winter wonderland, clean and bright and crisp. No matter what else happened on this trip, she was grateful for the snow, for the feeling of magic, even for a little while.

"Oh! Twirl me too!" Willow demanded and stretched out her arms for Poppy. The little girl was warm and snuggly when Rafe handed her into Poppy's arms. Willow had sugar on her lips, and her cheeks were red from the cold and the exertion.

"Did you get your car to the rental okay?" Adam asked. He slung his arm across Cassandra's shoulders and tucked her into his side. They'd finished hanging the lights.

"Yes, Rafe took me. And he took me to get a jacket and boots. Then we devoured the best pizza I've ever tasted in my life." She sneaked a glance at Rafe, who was eyeing her again with that confusing expression she couldn't understand. And damn, she wanted to know, so she smiled at him, thinking she'd maybe knock him off balance, make him give himself away. But it wasn't her that knocked him off balance.

Whomp. A snowball smacked Rafe in the shoulder. Miranda and Cruz laughed, a pile of snowballs at their feet.

"Snowballs!" Willow yelled. She kicked her feet to get down and Poppy let her go. Adam took Willow's tiny hand and helped her gather snow.

Cass snuggled Eli in her arms. "Come on, you, let's go be safe on the porch with the babies."

"My first snowball fight," Vivianna said, gave Jake a kiss and ran away laughing, picking up snow to make a ball.

Rafe stood still for a second, brushed his shoulder off, then casually bent and made a snowball. Then he ran toward Miranda and Cruz, but when he turned, he aimed directly for Poppy. The snowball hit her right in the chest. *Wow, he has good aim.* Laughter rang out behind her, then snowballs flew around them.

They slipped and played and threw snow. Cass and Eli watched from the porch. It was the perfect snow for little children like Willow—soft and fluffy, barely wet enough to make poofy snowballs that didn't hurt when they hit. Poppy hadn't laughed so hard in her life, dodging snowballs and tossing them at her cousins.

She blew on her fingers to warm them. They were red and raw and wet. One second she was watching the scene of fun and chaos and the next Rafe was falling into her. *Oof!* They landed in a snowbank, cocooned by the snow.

"So-sorry," Rafe said, his face inches from hers, his eyes inky pools she could get lost in. Eyes so beautiful they stunned her silent. She and Rafe stayed that way, unmoving in their quiet embrace, studying each other.

He had soft lines around his eyes, and she wondered if they were from hard work under the sunshine or laughter. Wondered what his laugh would sound like—deep and smoky maybe. Fantasized about how it would feel when he laughed against her lips.

She put her hand gently on his chest, not to push him off, but to feel him. They both froze in the moment. Rafe covered her hand with his own. That startled him out of whatever magical place they'd slipped into. "F-f-freezing. Your hands."

He stood and pulled her up. His were cold too, and so much bigger and thicker than hers. He had a scar on his thumb and rough calluses on a few fingers. Poppy sucked in a breath as he rubbed her hand in his. It hurt—her fingers really were frozen—but it also startled her into that same sharp awareness of her body, of Rafe standing so close and intently inspecting her fingers with his own, with his eyes, with his concern.

Her fingers might have been frozen, but her insides melted into a warm and gooey mess.

"Well," Miranda said. She was carrying Willow piggyback-style as she stomped up the porch steps. "We brought another surprise, apple cider and sonhos. Cass made them. They're deliciously addictive."

"Mm-hm, they're my true love." Adam patted his heart and swung Willow off Miranda's back.

"My true love," Willow mimicked. She was bundled in a snowsuit with puffy mittens, but even with the darling smile on her face, she shivered and yawned.

"Normally we wouldn't let ourselves in without an invitation," Cass said as they all shrugged out of their boots and winter jackets inside Rafe's living room. "But we wanted to heat the cider so you had something warm to come home to, and so it would scent the house. Plus, the donuts don't like to get cold."

"Please, we totally would have barged in to make sure you were okay, Rafe. You're family just as much as Poppy is," Miranda said. "Tell me you're not surprised. You've been here for what, decades?"

"Almost four years," Rafe answered.

"Well, it seems like you've always been here. You certainly belong."

Chapter Seven

Rafe wanted to keep holding Poppy's hands, heat them in his, maybe drift his fingers up her arm, under the sleeve of her shirt, see if her skin was as soft there as it was on her wrist, see if that part of her needed warming too. He was breathing hard from the exertion outside, or maybe it was from touching her. Three times he'd held her hand. He never wanted to let go.

Instead, trying to calm the racing inside his chest, he took her jacket and hung it in his new entry closet, then set their boots next to each other. When he turned back, she was staring at their boots. She reached her hand to her lips. When she caught his gaze, she didn't look away. That silent thread passed between them again. But it was like no silence he'd ever heard before. Slowly, her glasses fogged and she grinned. Instinct had him reaching out.

"Can I?" he asked.

She nodded and he took the frames and gently wiped them with the end of his flannel before he handed them back to her. She was so pretty with her glasses on. Smart, those frames said. *Confident.* Plus, they made her eyes pop. He saw a beautiful meadow when she cast those pretty green beauties on him. But without them, she was pretty too—younger, more vulnerable. Her right eye wanted to drift off to the side a bit, and her smile was wide, a tad lopsided. Freckles dotted her cheeks.

For a second, the look she gave him was so open and soft, tired, but true. He wanted to kiss her, kiss those plush lips and the pale skin, see if he could make her blush. Whoa. *Where did that come from?* Heat crept up his neck. He took a step back.

"Rafe, the place looks amazing!" Cass said. She had Willow and Eli on the couch and was rubbing their feet with her hands, tickling them at the same time. Willow's tiny husky laugh made him smile. "You need a dining room table for big family meals."

His smile faltered. He'd been quietly imagining family meals, maybe not huge ones. Now he'd never get to cook for his mother.

"I like the small one in this pretty corner nook," Poppy said.

She slid into the nook, onto the window bench he'd built. He'd built the small square table too, for himself. He'd planned on making a bigger one later. But that thought flew out of his mind. He liked her sitting there, making herself at home. She fit. She belonged. It heated his insides that she appreciated that small corner table. She blew on her hands and rubbed them together, caught him watching her and sent him a smile. Belonging had never been such a prominent place in his thoughts. Now the idea bounced around in his head, in his chest. His blood vibrated with the notion.

"You'll have to get Luca's help in the spring for landscaping," Jake said.

"You did good." Adam handed him a mug of cider and smacked his shoulder. "The black window frames were a great idea."

"I had help." He gave Adam a wry smile. His friends had been as much involved in the building of his place as he had. He couldn't have done it without their help. Or, he could have, but it would have taken him a year, maybe longer. Rafe set his mug on the mantel he'd built and started a fire. The heat from inside felt good on his body and a fire would add to that, and to the festivities. He'd been surprised to see them decorating his house when they'd arrived, and yet not really surprised at all. The Brockmans put their entire beings on the line to make people feel welcome, feel included. *Like family.*

"Yes, and it was so much fun. First our house, then Adam's house, your house. Who's next? Poppy?" Miranda brought a mug to Poppy and slid in beside her. "Please tell me you're moving to Graciella? I love that people are flocking back here."

"I...uhm...I'm not sure what I'm doing." Poppy shrugged. "I sort of left my life behind...and I came here because, well..."

"Your life in Paris?" Miranda asked gently.

Poppy nodded. There it was again, washing through her expression — anguish, despair? Rafe focused on the fire, unsettled by her emotions.

"What were you doing there?" Cruz asked. He set a platter of Cassandra's sonhos on the table. Mouthwatering donut holes covered in sugar.

"I was in fashion. I'm...well, I design clothes." She took a donut, tossing it gently between her fingers. Warm, sugar-coated, doughy and amazing.

"That *sounds* dreamy," Cass said. "But your expression says not so much."

Poppy swallowed and wiped her hands on the napkins Cass had set down. "No. And I'm pretty sure I ruined my career when I left."

"What happened?" Cruz asked.

Fear hovered in her expression, and Rafe wanted to step in and help her, but he just sat still and listened.

"I was meant to turn my designs in to my boss, but I didn't. I left and…I made it so I can never go back."

Cruz patted her hand. "I'm pretty sure you can always go back."

What Poppy hadn't said was that she didn't think she wanted to go back. At all. Maybe ever. Not to her tiny freezing apartment, not to her job, not to Paris, at least not while all the bad memories bubbled up to the surface. And maybe not even to design, which had once been her true love. A deep, aching loneliness shrouded it all, making it difficult to decipher what was important and what wasn't.

"Where's your mother, then?" Adam asked.

Willow was in his arms, her head on his shoulder. *Tired little puppy.* Poppy could empathize. Eli slept in his stroller and the other babies snoozed in theirs. Poppy was having trouble keeping her own eyes open.

"She's in New York mostly, sometimes Paris, and they, she and my stepdad, have a house in Hawaii too. They're busy, always needed somewhere." *So much so I've felt so adrift for so long I don't know how to anchor myself. Is that what this is all about? A place to feel stable, a foundation?*

"Did you leave them in Paris too?" Vivianna asked.

"No, no." Poppy shook her head. "They're in New York right now." *They don't know I'm here.* She glanced at Rafe again. He hadn't taken his gaze from her, and he gave no indication of what he was thinking. It felt like he could see right through her to all her secrets, all her failures.

"Well, I bet they're thrilled you're safe, and what a lovely place you have to stay in. Rafe's cottage, not a sacrifice at all, is it?" Miranda said.

"Uhm…"

"She's staying here," Rafe said. "I didn't get the furniture moved in before my…my mom died."

Oh. Oh no. She knew it. And it had just happened, apparently. And here she was all the way across the room from him and she wanted to be right next to him, wrapping her arms around him and saying all the right things, or nothing at all if he wanted peace and quiet. That vibration pulled at her, but it wasn't real, couldn't be real, could it?

"Jesus, I'm sorry," Adam said. "We dumped Poppy on you. I assumed her staying in your cottage would be okay, and I didn't even wait to hear back from you. Last night was chaotic with Willow crashing from too much sugar, the babysitter needing to get home and Lily going into labor. Not the way to treat a friend."

"It was no problem," Rafe said, shuttering his eyes from Poppy.

"He was very kind," she said. "He slept on the couch and made me coffee. I couldn't have asked for a nicer host. And I'm so sorry about your mom, Rafe."

He shook his head and she wished she knew what that meant. *It's okay. Thank you. I don't want to talk about it.*

"We have furniture in storage we bought for the renovated farm cottages that we haven't used," Miranda said.

"That's right. We could bring furniture by in the morning," Cruz added.

"Absolutely. It's the least we can do," Cass added.

"And Poppy," Miranda said, "we're having a big bake tomorrow morning at the main house. Naomi wants to make Christmas cookies and treats for the rehearsal dinner and wedding reception sweets table."

"That sounds great." She still needed to talk to her aunt, to ask the hard questions. That was what she should be focused on. Time to face the past, even if it would tear her apart. Her life was a mess anyway. Paris—her career had already fallen apart. It seemed like a good time to explode the rest of her life. She was either brave or stupid. Or weak because she was avoiding the whole thing.

"Here, give me your phone and I'll put our numbers in," Miranda said. "We should have thought of this last night."

God, her phone. She'd been avoiding her mother too. Where was her phone? It was dead, that was for sure, she hadn't charged it since she'd left Paris. She excused herself to run upstairs and grab it. It had been so nice not to be assaulted by the endless demands from her boss, or *ex-boss*, and her coworkers. Everyone taking from her all the time. Life happening in a rush, and her always a million steps behind. And cold. She'd been so damn cold in her tiny apartment, in her heart. *Oh, there it is, plugged in.* Poppy shook her head. Rafe must have done that for her.

Darn! Her phone had been busy again, this time with several missed calls from her mother. And even two texts. Her mother never texted, feeling it was too pedestrian.

Where are you? Poppy, call me now.

That was the extent of the texts. Maybe it was a good thing her mother refrained from the texting world. If there was a way to make people feel small and insignificant with as few words as possible, her mother had nailed it. Poppy would call her later when everyone was gone.

She flew back downstairs, to family, to laughter. Miranda put their contact information into Poppy's phone like a speedy digital wizard. She then dialed each number so the others had Poppy's number. "Great. Cruz and I are heading to the hospital to bring dinner to the new parents. We need to get going to pick up our sitter before that."

"And we've three sleepyheads on our hands," Adam said.

Willow was conked out on his shoulder, her little head nestled into his neck. She didn't even wake when Cass put her snowsuit on her. A floppy, precious doll dreaming happy dreams of sugared donuts and snowflakes. The twins had slept in their stroller the entire time. Everyone hugged and kissed her goodbye, gave Rafe hugs and suddenly it was the two of them again in the whoosh of quiet after so much hullabaloo. Poppy battled with whether to wish them all back or to relish what she and Rafe had now, because the quiet was nice too.

"They're all so lovely." Poppy sighed and hugged herself. She should have gotten a sweater or two as well. The house was warm, but the wind had sneaked in with their exit.

"They're your family."

"Well, yours too. Don't you think?" she asked him. *Oh shoot. Now there's a way to insert foot in mouth.* "I'm so sorry, I didn't mean… Gosh, I am so sorry about your mom, about your real family."

Rafe stared at the empty door, lost in thought, maybe pondering what she'd said. Had she messed up too badly? Her cousins and friends *did* adore and appreciate him. It was quite obvious. They were his found family, one he'd created all on his own, but no one could replace a mom. He opened his mouth but hesitated. She was beginning to recognize that pause of his. Then he blinked and turned away, picking up mugs and napkins on his way to the kitchen.

I should help him. Instead, Poppy shivered again and sank into the couch, tucking her feet under her. Suddenly jet lag curled around her. Her balance was off and all she could do was close her eyes from the force of it.

A family you make all on your own sounds glorious. Maybe she could be a part of her cousins' lives again. She yawned and rested her head on one of the throw pillows. *Ooo, lovely, soft.* Maybe Rafe could be a part of her life as well.

Poppy let sleep take her under. She drifted into dreams. Dreams of family, of a cozy house, of holding hands in the cold with an intense, quiet, kind man who stirred her heart into twirls.

Chapter Eight

Rafe carried the mugs to the sink. When he turned to gather the small plates on the coffee table, Poppy was curled in a ball, asleep on his couch. Even in sleep she was shivering. Wrapped around herself and working as hard as she could to keep her warmth in. Her face had softened, however, and the lines of worry that sprang up occasionally on her forehead were gone. He reached toward her face, hesitated, then, as carefully as he could, slid her glasses off, folded them closed and set them on the table in front of her.

He pulled out the large, chunky blanket Lily had made for him last month. Nesting, she'd called it, knitting hats and booties and baby blankets. When she'd finished those, she'd started on soft throw blankets for each of them. He gently covered Poppy with it and tucked the ends around her feet so none of the chill she was feeling could get through. In case she woke thirsty, he made her a cup of tea and set it beside her glasses.

It was tempting to watch her sleep, but that would be creepy. *Was* creepy. So he put on his jacket and headed to his workshop. His hands had been idle all day, except when he'd been holding Poppy's hand and throwing snowballs and lifting her up to warm her frozen fingers. Now empty, they itched to be working. Building or fixing, either would do. Calm his hands and his mind. Somehow, in a matter of hours, without her fingers linked with his, Rafe suddenly felt lacking.

His shop was as nice as many people's homes. Nicer, maybe. One enormous room, fully insulated, with heated cement floors, high ceilings and one big wide-open space. On his worktable were the designs for the new well he'd been designing for the farm. Every year, water got scarcer. The Brockmans had already done so much since TD Brockman had died. The idiot had nearly ruined the farm, not only financially but the health of the land. He'd abused it for so long, stripped it of all its nutrients, overwatered, overpoisoned.

Cruz and Adam had reduced the crops they grew, changed to more drought-tolerant ones, and, with Rafe's help, built a new irrigation system that wouldn't waste nearly as much water as the old sprayers had. But there was still more to be done to help the farm and the town of Graciella be sustainable. One couldn't survive without the other. It was a symbiotic relationship between the farm, all the neighboring farms and Graciella, and, even more simply, between man and nature. Humans couldn't survive without the land, and unfortunately humans were working as hard as they could to destroy it.

Rafe tried to get lost in his work. There'd be no drilling new wells now anyway, not for months. Hopefully the snow would continue, at least up north in the mountains, and rebuild the snowpack they'd lost in the last few years. Instead of designing, he took out the flat shelves he'd built out of walnut to go inside on what were now openings beside the fireplace.

He stirred the dark stain he'd fallen for because it reminded him of how tree bark turned in the rain — deep and rich with layers of texture. That was how he wanted the wood to appear when he was finished. Exactly like the beams he'd built for his living room ceiling. The stain was as sharp as the scent of snowfall in that it woke a person, but unlike the clean scent of fresh snow, this was harsh. Caustic almost.

Rafe dragged on his respirator and settled into the task of smoothing the rich stain over the wood. He worked it into the boards in a meditative push and pull. It changed each board from something unfinished and waiting to a gorgeous piece of art, whole and complete, useful and grand at the same time.

Carefully smoothing the stain over each crevice, catching the drips and going back over the parts where the stain had been too thick, Rafe worked until each board was perfect to his mind. The cracks and knots and all the grainy lines were sharp in contrast with one another now that the stain was setting. He thought of Poppy and the tiny freckles that stretched into her top lip, how her one eye wanted to cross and wander when she didn't have her glasses on, the wild untamed curls, her uncertainty of where she belonged.

Maybe all those layers were like the walnut now, exposed for its true self, its true worth, all her imperfections making her beautiful in his mind, making her Poppy. He thought about himself and wondered if another soul could see him that way, with all his faults and all the harsh grainy lines, and still maybe love him. Everyone kept offering their condolences about his mother, but what would they say, how would they look at him if they knew she'd never really wanted him? That these people he'd only known for four years really were more like family to him than his own mother?

Disturbed and with his concentration shot, Rafe washed his hands and stood contemplating what to do next, but his mind was blank. What he wanted was to check on Poppy, see if she was still asleep, see if she needed anything.

* * * *

"What?" Poppy shot upright and blinked the sleep out of her eyes. Her face was hot where it had been plastered to the pillow. Her hair was probably a mess, but she was warm now. She noticed the blanket on her and tugged it closer around her shoulders. It was soft and heavy. It made her feel hugged. Her phone buzzed on the coffee table next to her glasses. Another one of those charming insulated mugs with a top sat there too. Poppy smiled at the thought of Rafe making her another drink and taking care of her. Her smile fell when she saw her mother's name on the phone. Taking a deep breath, she answered.

"Hi, Mom."

"Poppy. Where have you been? I've left messages. For Pete's sake, I even texted, hoping that ridiculousness would get your attention. How are your designs coming? What did Jean Pierre say? Did they make the cut?"

All the warmth slithered out of Poppy's body and she curled into the blanket to seek its protection. She couldn't hide anymore, couldn't run. She was tired of it all anyway, the fear, the need to escape. *You're safe now, far, far away from Jean Pierre.* He couldn't touch her here. She needed to keep reminding herself of that. She might have ruined her career, she might not have a life to go back to, but he couldn't get to her anymore. Never again.

She rubbed her forehead. "No, they didn't make the cut. I didn't submit them, not completely." She had given Jean Pierre a glimpse at work one morning, after he'd repeatedly come by her desk and tried to inspect them. She'd thought it would get him off her back, if he could see how hard she'd been working, that she was almost finished. It only made him more focused on her, and not in the way she'd thought she wanted — the boss, the great designer taking the younger one under his wing to mentor.

No, he'd leered at her. *"Très bien, ma petite,"* he'd said as he snaked his finger along her neck. It was the second time he'd touched her when she hadn't anticipated it, when she hadn't *asked for it,* when she hadn't wanted him to. Both times at work, and she'd frozen, because there were people around eyeing her — her coworkers, her competitors. As it turned out, none of them her friends.

"What?"

Her mother's shock brought her back to the present. Poppy took in her surroundings. The fire still burned, although not as hot as before. Scents of cinnamon and cider lingered in the air. Her body rested against soft couch cushions. It was quiet, peaceful.

"You didn't finish them? You're still working on them? What's going on?"

"They're mostly finished," she answered, because it was the truth. "But I didn't give them to Jean Pierre. He wanted…he wanted too much. I couldn't…" The words got stuck in the fear of what might have happened had she stayed. "I left. I left Paris and my job." There, the words might have been stilted and frozen in ice, but she'd said them. Let her mom be disappointed. Poppy could handle it, hopefully.

"Poppy, what is going on?" her mother demanded. "You don't simply leave such a great opportunity. You've worked too hard to quit. He wanted too much? What do you mean? There are sacrifices to be made to be the best. And you're the best. Wait, did you say you left Paris? Where are you?"

"I'm in Graciella." Wow, she was twenty-seven years old and she'd finally figured out how to silence her mother. The small hiss of the fire logs startled her. "Mom?"

"I don't understand. You left your job that you've put everything into."

Poppy had put everything into her fashion dream. So much so that she questioned if she had anything left. Because her career, her so-called dream had sucked the life from her. Empty was one word to describe her, hollowed out, completely exhausted from the competitiveness, the non-stop work, the back-stabbing people she'd surrounded herself with. Where had her love of design gone, her joy in sewing gorgeous clothes, her creativity?

"Yes," she whispered, unaware if her mother could hear her or not.

"We've never been impulsive," her mother said as if the two of them had teamed up to banish such an annoyance, a mosquito in one's face.

Poppy had never been good enough for her mother. She'd never measured up completely and she knew she never would. And she was tired. Tired of trying to change who she was or what she really loved to please her mother. Because it hadn't made Poppy happy, and it would never, ever happen, the pleasing of Anne Emilia Bergstrom. "What were you thinking? That it was too difficult? It's worth it, all the sacrifices you make now. We've talked about this."

"Should I have sacrificed my body? Is that part of the business? Because that's what it came to, Mom. My designs were finished. And they were good, or so I thought. And he called me into his office and said he'd choose me, choose my designs to feature at the show, make my career, send it soaring. Sounds wonderful, doesn't it? Grand and exciting. All I had to do was sleep with him."

"Poppy." Her mother's voice sounded so far away. It was. *She* was. She always had been, even when they were in the same room in the same house in the same city. "I don't... I can't..." her mother stuttered.

"And I said no."

"Oh, honey," her mother said, and Poppy didn't pause at her mother's soft tone.

"So he found out where I lived, surprised me at the door of my apartment." Poppy's tears began to fall then, and the cold slithered through her body, but she forced herself onward. "I told him to leave and he wouldn't, tried to put his hands on me and..."

"*God*, Poppy."

"I shoved him, and my neighbor came out and scared him away, old Madam Etienne and her scary one-hundred-year-old cat and her cigarettes and her cane. But he knew where I lived, and he came back that night, tried to open my door. For two weeks I slept with the lights on or, well, I didn't sleep much. I hardly left my apartment, only when I knew he'd be gone on one of his trips. Then I found a flight, packed what I could and I left. I know I disappointed you, but I couldn't stay. I couldn't."

"You didn't disappoint me. You never do. I'm so sorry. I'm so sorry." There was sincerity in her mother's tone, although it was difficult to reconcile with the words, *"You didn't disappoint me. You never do."* How could that be? Her whole life had been one action after another trying to make sure she didn't disappoint her mother.

"I wish you'd called us. I wish you'd come home, darling."

"Where is my home, Mom? I love you and Will, but I've never felt at home in the high-rise apartment in New York. *You* love it, but it's not mine. It never was." Poppy looked up to find Rafe standing in the doorway from the back porch to the kitchen, his arms full of firewood, his cheeks flushed from the cold, dark eyes studying her. Suddenly she felt exposed and exhausted and defeated.

"But Graciella? Really?" Her mother interrupted her thoughts. "I—"

"Yes, Mom. It was impulsive, but it felt necessary." She didn't have the energy to explain why she'd really come to Graciella. That would take heaps more than she had at the moment. One crisis at a time was all she could handle. "I'm here and I'm okay and I'm sorry I didn't call you. And I need to go now, but I'll call you tomorrow. I love you."

And she hung up before her mother could say anything else.

Chapter Nine

Sometimes — oh, who was he kidding? *Always* — it took Rafe eons to say what he wanted. Often, he didn't speak at all. He'd learned a lot about people and the world from being quiet anyway. He'd learned to listen to the waves against the shore to recognize when a storm might be coming, or the sound of the fire as it petered out. How the air smelled when frost might come and ruin early crops. He listened to what people said and what they didn't. Often what they didn't say was the truth, or louder anyway than what they'd actually said. *Do people think that about me?*

He'd also learned to read people's expressions. That was difficult too, because people created many masks to hide behind. But not Poppy. She didn't hide anything with her words or her expressions. And right now, her face said so many things — disgust, pain, worry. Like she was lost in a storm with no bearings and no coat or gloves, with no one to save her, to help her. He wanted to be that person for her, that steady light in the storm.

But he was gripped by an emotion he was mostly unfamiliar with. He had to work at it, banking the anger that surged inside him at her words. A man had tried to hurt her. Deep red emotions surged through his blood, so harsh he felt it pulsing, clawing.

Rafe rarely got angry. Instead, he got to work. He'd learned long ago to bank his dangerous emotions, focus his mind, retreat into his own thoughts and space, to challenge himself. Now the challenge was different, live and viral. He wanted to yell and charge at whoever had dared hurt her.

He took a step closer and noticed her tear-stained face, so pale now that even her freckles had faded with her anguish. And his anger seeped out, replaced by a different grip on his heart causing it to beat erratically. It felt like losing his breath and finding it all over again in the same second.

Are you – "Okay?" he managed to ask.

"I don't know," she answered. She wiped off her face, set her glasses down and took the mug he'd left for her. "Better now." She sipped the tea and faced him. "Thank you for the tea and the blanket and for taking my glasses off. I fall asleep with them on too often, my mom says. That was my mom. I guess…maybe you could tell."

He nodded. She must be okay at least if she could talk. How did he say she could talk to him, that he wanted to listen? Rafe set the firewood by the fire and sat gently on the couch, leaving space between them. "S-s-someone hurt you?"

He didn't know whether to face her or not. If she was embarrassed, maybe she wouldn't want him to notice, but when he took a quick glance, she was staring with that wide openness again. Exposed without her glasses on, with her eyes red and the dark circles underneath.

"He tried," she said and took a sip of tea. Then she tucked her knees up to her chest and, shrugging the blanket closer around, faced him. "He was my boss. A horrible man and he... I'm a fashion designer. I was supposed to turn in my designs to him, and he threatened to not use them in the collection, even though..." She took a huge breath. "Even though I've been working on them for months. Unless I...well..."

Poppy's face was red now with her embarrassment. Rafe didn't want her to feel that. She shouldn't feel bad for what some asshole had done.

"But..." She swallowed and spoke more strongly now. "He didn't get me, and I left. I ran away from my life, my job, my apartment."

"Someone scares you or th-th-threatens you, that's hurting y-you." Dammit, his nerves beat out of control in his body. His blood felt hot, then cold. He sealed his mouth shut.

Poppy stared at him. *Is she searching for answers? What does she see?* She nodded and gave him a small, tired smile.

"Yeah, you're right," she whispered.

Rafe wanted to take her hand, feel the caress of her soft skin connected to his, twine their fingers together. He wanted to hold her, protect her, but he was confused as to whether or not he should. Just because he wanted to touch her didn't mean she'd welcome it. Especially now after she'd told him what had happened to her. She might never want his touch. And he didn't have a clue how to ask her those things. Now wasn't the time to be entertaining those thoughts. He stood, fidgeting with all the feelings whipping through his body.

"Hungry?"

"You're always feeding me," she said. And her voice had lost its dark edges of misery.

"I… It's what… It's something I can do. It's dinnertime."

"No, I like it. I can't remember the last time someone made me a meal or made sure I got fed or that I was warm." She rubbed her hand on the throw blanket. "Taken care of."

Poppy met his gaze and smiled again, and when the organ in his chest flipped over with joy, he knew he was in trouble.

"That's…that's how I feel here, with you."

Like an idiot, he stood there, the urge to go to her, to wrap her up so strong he… His space was flipped around. And he was spinning in it, unbalanced.

"I'm not a good cook, not good at all, or I'd help you. Would you mind if I got my sewing machine out?"

Rafe normally cooked alone, and he enjoyed it, but now images of cooking in his kitchen next to Poppy flooded his mind, seeing her smile, feeling her body brush against his, surrounded by the scent of her, floral and sweet. Who cared if she couldn't cook? They might even ruin a meal together. And suddenly he didn't think he'd mind that at all.

"Rafe?"

"Huh? Sure." He turned, hoping she hadn't been able to read his mind, see his thoughts. He was supposed to be making her feel comfortable. If he was lusting after her, he'd sure better keep that to himself.

Rafe handed her a knife to open her box and tried to ignore her while he studied the contents of his refrigerator. He'd need to go shopping soon. The fridge mostly had a few condiments and the things Katie had brought over for Poppy. He had a few vegetables and frozen tortellini. Soup would do for now.

Pretending to ignore her didn't mean he wasn't aware of what she was doing. It made him hyperaware. He wanted to help her lift her machine out, but she was capable of doing it herself. Logic didn't matter. He wanted to be by her side, to have the right to be by her side.

He tried not to notice while she carefully lifted out what she'd packed around it, fabrics folded tightly, a black one, an iridescent light green the same color as her eyes, another that was covered in shimmering gold. She draped them over the couch, running her hands over them like they were cherished and she was making sure they'd survived their long, dark journey. Then he nearly cut himself as her smile bloomed when she lifted the machine from the box. Rafe set the knife on the cutting board and took a deep breath.

"Oh, you don't have an iron, do you?" She laughed. "I'm sure you don't. Oh well, maybe Aunt Katie will have one. I'll ask her tomorrow. In the meantime, I might sew a few seams on a dress I've been making. Actually, I haven't been working on it at all." Poppy sighed and carried her machine to the small table in the front nook. "I've had this horrible block for the last few months, but now I have all these ideas running through my head of things I want to finish, new items I want to make. It's going to feel so good to rediscover my creative energy, you know."

"Hm," he said and managed to get the vegetables into the pot to simmer without any injuries. Her soft voice soothed him, even if he didn't have much to say in response. Salt went in next, and he stirred and nestled the leeks and garlic over the hot oil.

"That smells amazing," she said.

He risked a glance her way, and she was studying him with that soft vulnerability again.

"My, uh, my apartment in Paris didn't have a real kitchen, only a small hot plate and a fridge the size of my pinky." She fiddled with her sewing machine.

Rafe poured the broth in, and the scent took on more nuances.

"Oh my gosh. You're killing me," she said, and it made his mouth quirk.

She'd eaten half the pizza on her own at lunch, plus donuts and cider. He'd want to cook for her whenever she asked. It had been a long time since he'd cooked for anyone, maybe ever, aside from his mother when he visited her. And he could never really tell if his mom liked what he made. Her mind had always been miles away.

Rafe studied Poppy. She'd moved to the kitchen island to watch him. Then he put a small bowl of olives in front of her, grabbed the box of crackers and a package of salami and set those on the island as well. The soup would take at least an hour. He got out a small plate in case she wanted to take some snacks back to the table with her.

"Thank you."

Her broad smile shocked him again. Luckily for their meal and his fingers, she turned away and took them to her corner. It was a battle to calm his racing heart again. Much easier than reining in his libido, which was acting like a caged lion, a hungry caged lion. He focused on his cooking and only allowed his mind to wander to Poppy working in her corner a few times.

He might be uncomfortable with how he felt, how he wanted her, but it was also nice, the quiet and them both working in the same space. She was there—her warmth, her scent...even the way she mumbled to herself.

Rafe wanted to stay in this space forever with her here beside him, not *his*, theirs, one they created and inhabited together. That thought was a rush to his head. Images flashed to him of her being his, of belonging to her.

"You're always feeding me," she'd said. *No, but I want to be that person, the one who feeds you, who makes your eyes brighten merely by sautéing leeks in butter, the one who cares for you.*

"Oh no." A hushed exclamation came from the nook. "My machine got broken during the flight."

When he walked up beside her, there was her sweet scent again, making him dizzy. He rested his hands on the table to steady himself. A small circular knob on the top right was bent or perhaps broken.

"Can I?" he asked before he ran his hands over her machine.

Poppy nodded and leaned in closer to him as he inspected it.

"I can f-f-fix this." *Get yourself under control, idiot.* Deep breaths weren't working. Talking himself into a calm place wasn't working. Being near her busted all his carefully practiced techniques into smithereens.

Fixing things didn't require speech. He stood and put out his hand to help her. "Here," he said. She took it and it was too late for him to worry whether touching her was right or not because she hadn't wavered, but instead put her hand right into his, like she trusted him. He shrugged on his coat, held hers out for her, lifted the machine and gestured for her to follow him out to his workshop.

"Wow," she said as soon as she set foot inside.

Damn, her husky awe sang through his blood.

"This is as beautiful as your house. You built this too, didn't you?" She ran her hands along the wall of shelves where he hung his tools, organized so he could grab what he needed without confusion.

He hadn't thought of his shop as beautiful, just necessary. But he had loved building it, knowing it was for him to create and fix things with his hands. Pride filtered through him. He wanted to ask her what she appreciated about it, hear her tell him in that sweet voice of hers.

"The beams are absolutely gorgeous. They look a hundred years old. Even here, these pieces are lovely." She ran her hands along the rows of random cuts of wood he'd slid into the vertical dividers.

She answered his desires without him even asking and he didn't understand his feelings around that either. Emotions bubbled inside him.

"All this beautiful wood, waiting for you to create beautiful things. And these, what are these?"

"Don't." Rafe grabbed her hand before she reached the shelves he'd stained earlier.

"Oh, sorry." She pulled away and he was instantly annoyed at himself at the way her face shuttered.

"No. I'm. I'm…sorry." He gently took her hand and set one of her fingers upon the wood. "Still wet."

Understanding bloomed in her eyes and she smiled as she inspected the dark stain on her finger. Then he took a work rag and, holding her hand, wiped the stain off her skin as much as he could. His body heated at how close they were standing. He focused on the task because he could feel her eyes on him and he was afraid of what she might see in his. *Coward.*

"Rafe?" She gripped the hand that was holding hers and took a step even closer, then reached out and cupped his cheek.

Her cold fingers felt good on his hot skin, soothing where he ached. He ached all over. For her. Feeling brave or stupid or both, he dragged his gaze to hers and what he saw was pure beauty casting her shine on him.

"You create stunning things. I'm sure people tell you that all the time, but I…I wanted to say it too."

He shook his head and covered her hand on his cheek with his own, letting her warmth seep through him completely. "No."

"No, you don't? Or no people don't say?" Her scrunched-up expression said she didn't believe either ridiculous notion. Where had she come from? Swooping in with her light and her belief and her scent wrapping around him.

He shook his head. How did he explain? "People don't say." He wanted to admit to the other too, that he created what he saw in his mind, that they weren't beautiful or stunning, they were just *right*, according to him. Only his pulse was thundering so fast, and for one tiny moment he wanted to believe what she said, let it sing through him, hold it tight so he could bring it out and savor it again after she left. When she was gone and all he had remaining of her was this feeling right now.

"Well, people are stupid, that's for sure," she said, and he huffed out a laugh. How certain she was of her statement.

"Whoa!" Her mouth fell open, and she took her hand from his and traced it around his lips.

God, she had him so turned on in an instant that he wanted to pull those long, graceful fingers of hers into his mouth while his gaze held hers to see if they lit on fire. He wanted to crowd her against the table and — stained shelves be damned — kiss her everywhere. Kiss her surrounded by his work and the scent of wood and sawdust while their bodies connected.

"Did you…? Are you…? Is that a smile?"

She was teasing him. Even being playful was something she managed to make sexy. Dizziness swirled inside him again.

"Rafe?" she whispered again, his name on her lips.

Her voice drifted over him, a soft cloud, a feather tantalizing the hair on his skin in awareness of her.

"Are you going to…? Do you want…?" Her whispered words trailed off as she studied his lips.

"Want." It was a statement, not a question. Couldn't she tell how much he *wanted*? His hands weren't clever or sure now. They shook with desire for her — to hold her close, so close so that no matter what, she couldn't leave, wouldn't ever dream of going.

Slowly, he placed his shaking hands on her hips. The feel of her burned him and it was all he could do not to haul her against him, but he didn't. She needed to be able to move away if she chose. But she looked into his eyes and there it was, a lock clicking into place. They were both caught in it. She stood on her tiptoes, and he shivered at the sweep of her body dragging against his.

"Can I kiss you?" Her voice was so soft, a plea.

She brushed her fingers across his lower lip and an ache rushed through his body. He was breathing heavily. *So is she. Beautiful woman.* Her body arched into his with each inhale and exhale. When she darted her eyes up to his again — those meadows of green through soft, long lashes—and he caught the emotions, vulnerability mixed with desire, he kept her gaze locked in his and slid one hand slowly around to her back. To make a memory of that too, of each second she stood there in his arms, to hold her there, hold them both steady.

With gentle pressure, he brought her flush against him and nodded. Slightly, her eyes changed, darkened, her lips parted, and he thought he heard a soft "oh" of surprise or delight. Although it was difficult to tell over the roaring in his body. She stood there, staring at him, frozen too, like she couldn't look away, didn't dare. Their hearts beat against each other. His was trying to climb out of his chest to meet hers, to feel it bare against him, to capture the beat of hers and wrap it up in his.

He wanted the kiss, but this was enough to make his blood hum, to wake him from a lifetime of deep, dreamless sleep. A heated embrace with her eyes changing color the more she felt, the more they both felt. The silent messages passed between them without even the hint of a kiss. Or maybe there was. Maybe this was the hint, the before, the longing. When they both sensed how special it was. This was unlike any kiss he'd anticipated before.

How had he missed this before space in the other kisses he'd had? This moment wrapped in each other's arms, this place of being one? When she touched his lips again, he couldn't tell if she was nervous or the most sensual creature he'd ever encountered.

"Poppy?" he said, and there was no stutter. It felt right to say her name before they kissed, the beauty of it. And also for her to know he saw her, he wanted her too. "You're sure?" No matter how dangerous the edge of his desire was, he knew in that moment he would do anything for her, even if it meant stepping away.

Then it was her lashes fluttering closed and open, the way she sighed into him that sent him soaring right before she set her smooth lips upon his. Soaring until she made contact. Then it was an explosion of feeling. He gripped her to him as if she might float away, walked them against his workbench and savored her mouth. Her soft caress went from slow and wondering to hot and needy in a matter of seconds. She tugged his head closer and, on an inhale, opened her mouth and let him feast, their tongues tangling, bodies close, so close.

The scent of her, soap and wildflowers, flew around him. He lifted her to sit on his table and she opened her legs to let him fit right into her. Rafe had never been shocked by a kiss before, but now electricity zapped through his blood, urging him on. He tasted her lips, kissed along her jaw, let his fingers appreciate the soft skin along her neck. She tugged at his shirt, trailed her fingers to the bare skin along his back, and he practically growled at the feeling.

She seemed as desperate, rubbing against him, nipping at his ear, until she found her way to his mouth, closed her eyes and kissed him again. He kept his eyes wide open. He wasn't going to miss one second of watching her. How she fit against him. The way her cheeks flushed. How his kisses left her neck rosy and marked.

When she opened her eyes, she paused, but didn't pull away. Instead, she smiled against his mouth like she couldn't believe how amazing this kiss was either. Slowly, after one more tug of his bottom lip, she did pull away, not too far, but enough that their mouths were no longer dancing. Their chests heaved in the quiet air. Her smile was shy and she rested her forehead against his chest.

"Wow. Wow, wow," she whispered.

He hummed, completely incapable of speech at the moment and maybe ever again. Rafe cradled her head with one hand and ran the other over her back to steady them both with the motion. "Soup's almost ready," he said like an idiot. Because soup was what every woman wanted to hear about after giving him the kiss of a lifetime.

Chapter Ten

"Poppy, you're right on time, love. I still can't believe you're here and that you've stayed even though we've hardly gotten to visit." Aunt Katie pulled her into a hug.

Poppy held on longer than normal. Yes, she'd missed hugs. "I'm so glad to be here. Rafe's been very kind. He walked me over." He hadn't held her hand, but he'd walked close, and she'd thought maybe he'd wanted to as much as she had, their fingers grazing against one another like a big tease, heat zapping between them even through the chill in the air.

Either that or she was fooling herself into a fairy-tale situation because it was so beautiful and peaceful here, with the snow-covered landscape and her heart floating on a beautiful cloud.

They hadn't talked on the walk either, simply enjoyed the stillness. He'd given her a nod and an almost-smile when she'd left him at the kitchen door and thanked him. He'd hesitated like he'd wanted to say something, to kiss her again. She'd been certain he could hear her thoughts echoing that sentiment. She hadn't hurried him, but in the end, he'd held his hand up in a small wave and walked away.

As she spent more time with him, she was learning his silences held meaning, and she didn't want to always be barging in, demanding he speak. She sure did wonder if he wanted to kiss her again though, as desperately as she wanted him to.

Now she was ushered into the busy warmth of the kitchen and her mind was forced to face other things. *Holy crap, another cooking situation!* It wasn't that she didn't enjoy others cooking or baking—she just wasn't any good at it. At all. The kitchen at Brockman House was fluttering with people, mostly women. Miranda, Cass and little Willow, next to two other little girls, Vivianna, Aunt Katie, a few others she didn't recognize. She remembered the bride and groom from her first night here. A few new male faces. And there were Christmas cutout cookies all over the place. Some going into the oven, others coming out, tons cooling on racks. Piping bags, frosting and sprinkles littered the tables.

"Hi, Poppy, I'm Gabby. I don't know if you remember me—"

"Oh, my goodness, Gabby Flores?" Poppy was enveloped in another hug. Long-hidden memories flooded her mind. "We used to play salon and you'd fix all our hair and makeup. It's so good to see you." *Friends.* A very long time ago, Poppy had had family and friends surrounding her. Who else had she forgotten, let go on the wind?

Gabby let her go and laughed. "I remember. I gave everyone perms because they wanted curly hair like yours. Guess what? Now I have my very own salon in downtown Graciella. Can you believe it?"

Gabby's joy was contagious. Poppy nodded. "Without a doubt. I always knew you would be successful. You were always so focused."

"I can't wait to catch up with you while you're here. I'd love to show you my salon too, if you have time before you leave."

Poppy didn't want to go anywhere. *Could I stay right here with all of you? All of you wonderful people from my past, and Rafe too. He could be my future.* The thought sang through her.

Last night had been delightful and excruciating at the same time. Delightful because Rafe had cooked for her. More than that, he'd fed her, and fixed her sewing machine like a super magician. Then he'd let her take over that corner of his house with her sewing, and he'd seemed content in all of it.

After dinner, she'd pinned together all the pieces of a dress she'd dreamed about but hadn't touched since last summer. Had it really been that long since she'd sewn for pleasure? Rafe had put on an old Johnny Cash record and read while she sewed, and one by one, her worries about Paris and her life had eased into a softer space in her mind.

The man could cook. His mushroom soup was the best she'd ever had. And the toasted bread he'd made to dip in it with the garlic and parmesan... Poppy thought she'd entered food paradise. He'd even gotten snacks out for her before dinner, probably because her grumbling stomach had echoed throughout the room. But more than that, he'd created a lovely space to simply exist in. When her eyes had started to blur over, she'd realized he'd fallen asleep on the couch with his book about global water shortages on his chest. She'd dragged herself to bed, a tiny bit disappointed there hadn't been any more kissing.

Poppy brushed her fingers over her lips. She could still feel his searing kiss branded on her. A flush rose up her neck at the memory.

"Come sit and pick your poison," Miranda said, interrupting her fantasies. "You can cut out cookies that still need to be baked or start decorating."

Neither of those sound too out of my league. Poppy slid into the booth next to Cass. Willow was on Cass' other side, sitting in a booster seat, using a plastic knife to spread icing over a Santa cookie. Her cute face was serious and intent and she had green icing on her lip. The two little girls — twins, Poppy could see now — sat with her, decorating their own cookies.

This was all so lovely. She was deliciously warm, the kitchen smelled fantastically of sugar and coffee, and Poppy relaxed into the moment. "Cutting out cookies sounds delightful. It's been a while." Maybe she'd ease into the decorating bit. After all, she loved drawing and creating designs with color, and she, Gabby and Lily had drawn through a gazillion sketch books when they were little.

Katie brought her coffee. Conversation and laughter filtered around her and Poppy tried to imagine this was her place, here surrounded by family and love and holiday traditions. *I want to stay, to belong here.* It was a fierce thought, tightening in her chest, clear as the icy crystals dangling from the apple tree branches.

"Tell us all about Paris," Aunt Katie said. "Poppy's been studying and working in fashion design in Europe." Happiness bloomed on her cheeks at her aunt's pride. But the shame quickly followed, roiling in her stomach.

"That sounds fabulous. I love Paris. I bet you met the most amazing people. I'd live there if I could afford it." Grant was Cass' friend from San Francisco. He was married to Drake and Poppy instantly adored both of them. They'd hugged her that first night here upon introductions as if they'd known her for years. Grant was currently decorating snowflake cookies like a professional cookie decorator and Poppy could have watched him for hours.

"It is expensive," she said. "To live there." So, so expensive. Her tiny apartment certainly wasn't what most people envisioned when they dreamed of Paris' beauty and charm. Charming wasn't freezing to death at night and having her plumbing not work more often than it did. And she'd met more lovely people this week in Graciella than she had for two years in Paris. *Probably because I worked like a slave. Ha, fitting, since I lived in old servant quarters.*

"Were you there all by yourself?" Cass asked. "That could be fabulous or lonely, I suppose."

"Yes," Poppy said. "I worked all the time, so I didn't really have time to make friends or sightsee. It was… Work was overwhelming hours, and my job was…it was horrible, now that I think about it. I mean, I knew it was horrible at the time." The words spilled out of her. "But sometimes you keep going, assuming things will get better or in too much of a fog to realize they never will, right? Then your boss tries to…well demand *things* in exchange for your designs being promoted, so you run away and ruin your career, your life."

Except ruined wasn't how she felt. Poppy looked up from her task of cutting out star shapes. Everyone had stopped what they were doing and stared at her.

"Cookie?" Willow asked and handed it to Poppy.

What could she do? She accepted the offering and took a bite. "Sorry," she said and swallowed. "I didn't mean to spill all of that. You make a lovely environment here."

"Honey." Katie covered Poppy's hand with her own. "That sounds awful. Are you okay? Does your mom know all of this?"

Poppy smiled. "I'm better now." *So much better.* "It feels so good to be here. I talked to my mom last night." She looked around and caught the stares. "Oh shoot, I'm so sorry. Didn't mean to dampen the festivities."

"Oh hush," Maggie, another friend of Cass', said. "I'm glad you got that off your chest. I'm so sorry all of that happened to you. And I think I can say for all of us that we're happy you're here."

"Yes," Katie said. "I'm so glad you thought to come here, Poppy."

* * * *

Morning turned to afternoon, and the loveliness continued. Cozy, happy. It was a revelation. People trickled in and out of the kitchen. Suddenly the only ones left were Poppy and her aunt. They'd just finished eating hot grilled cheeses and potato chips. All the salty goodness after too many cookie taste tests was perfect. Although the tastings had been so much fun.

"I'm glad it's just us, Poppy. I've missed you so much."

"Me too, Aunt Katie."

"It was all so horrible when you left. And your mother wanting a clean slate, which I totally understand."

And my father not wanting me. The words burned through her. *How do I let that old ache go? Will I ever be able to?* How did one deal with such a thing? It was etched into her soul. Katie was her dad's sister — maybe she could shed light on Poppy's questions, if she was brave enough to ask.

"Selfishly, I wish she'd let me keep in touch with you and that she hadn't pulled so far away. I knew she was hurting. I guess I didn't comprehend how much, lost in my own drama at the time, in all the heartbreak. She was angry too. And she had every right to be. I suspected that's why she didn't bring you back for the funeral. And I never got to say how sorry I was. You were so young. We...we all failed you."

Ice shivered through her veins. She set her tea down. "The funeral?"

"Your father's."

"What?" Poppy whispered. "When...his funeral? I thought...I thought he was still alive. It's why...why I came back." Her throat had gone dry, and an agonizing pressure squeezed the breath from her lungs.

"Oh, God," Katie said, and her face paled. "You didn't know? How could...how could...oh dear Lord, Annie never told you? And she cut off communication with me. Oh Poppy, I'm sorry. He died right after you left. One week later. He was in a car accident."

The words barreled toward her through a tunnel, loud and furious. "No." She was shaking her head, trying to knock the words away, to deny them.

"Poppy. I'm so sorry."

"I..." She struggled to stand. Her legs shook. Grabbing her jacket, she shrugged her arms through the sleeves and nearly tripped putting her boots on. "I have to go."

"Honey, please stay. I've upset you. I had no idea." Katie reached out.

"No..." She was trying to keep it together, but she needed to get outside, to move, to run. "I'm not mad at you. I...I need to...to think...to call my mother." And she ran out of the door. The bracing cold air slammed into her lungs, lungs that felt as though they could barely find any oxygen. What she could find was a harsh, bitter emotion slithering through her. She kept running through the orchards with their sparkly limbs, her boots crunching over snow that had started to melt and freeze again, across the fields to Rafe's house. Running out her confusion while her heart broke into a thousand pieces. She made it through the front door, tracking snow all over as she forgot to take off her boots. She had to call her mother.

Her phone was plugged in on the kitchen island. Rafe must have done it for her again. She was horrible at remembering to charge it. It had been so nice to be here in Graciella where she didn't have to worry about it so much. There were two missed calls from her mother but when she dialed it went right to voicemail.

God, *God*. Her father was dead? *How could I never have known? All these years?* Her surroundings came into focus. She was alone. There was a trail of melting snow on the floor. Absentmindedly she thought she should clean it up, but her body refused to match her thoughts. Noise filtered in from outside and she followed it, her body tight and...and angry. She forced herself out through the back door to see her cousins and Rafe unloading furniture into the cottage.

"Hey, Poppy!" Adam called, his smiling face flushed. "We outfitted the cottage for you. Bedroom, living room, dining room, and Miranda even had plates and stuff for the kitchen. Now you'll have the whole charming place all to yourself."

"Oh." *What?* Her breathing was heavy from the running. "Thank you." Manners had her answering, engaging, an alien inside of her responding.

"I'm going to head home to Lily. Roxanna stopped by to visit the baby. I don't want to leave them too long in case they need me." Turner gave Poppy a quick hug.

"Congratulations," she said. The word came and she was half amazed she was able to speak at all over the roaring in her head.

"Holler if you want to come by and meet the newest Brockman. He's the cutest thing you've ever seen." Turner looked exhausted and gloriously happy at the same time.

"Heard you all had a great time decorating cookies for the wedding. Willow talked herself to sleep telling me all about it. I've got to head off too." Adam turned and jogged up the hill.

She stood there, shivering in the cold as sweat now chilled against her skin. Adrenaline had swept through her, leaving her weak and confused. Rafe stood on the porch, his gaze on her. She made her way up the steps and inside, like a good girl, doing what she was supposed to do, one foot in front of the other, her body iced over, her heart numb.

"Are you o-okay?"

A sharpness laced his words. It came to her on a wobbly brush of air. The world around her was unbalanced and she needed to sit, to call her mother again. She needed to speak... She needed to ask...

She turned away. "I'm not feeling too well. Jet lag maybe. It...uhm..." Poppy couldn't remember what she was saying or what she should say.

Poppy looked around at the furniture, not making sense of anything. Rafe didn't say anything and neither did she. The wind whispered between them. Eventually he moved down the steps, never taking his eyes off her, until finally he let out a long breath, turned and made his way to his own house. *Come back to me. Hug me, please,* she wanted to beg. *Hold on and don't ever let me go. I don't know how to say what's happening inside me.* But the words were lost in the pain in her stomach, churning.

She closed the door then sank against it, her butt hitting the hardwood floors. A lovely pair of soft gray sofas sat in front of the fire. They'd even put a fluffy rug there. It would be comfy for the feet. A wood dining table and chairs were there as well, with a vase in the center full of winter branches. Everything where it should be. And her alone again, exactly how she'd always been. A state she'd hoped and prayed she wouldn't have to be forever. That somewhere around the corner, or the next job, or assignment she'd find her place, where she felt whole, where she belonged *with* someone.

Her hand was shaking when she fumbled with her phone. Her mother's name flashed on the screen. "Mom."

"Poppy. I've been trying to call you again. I've been so worried."

"You lied to me." The words were shoved out of her mouth, caustic and biting.

"What? Poppy, what are you talking about?"

"Dad. You never told me..." She could barely get the words out. "He died. He's *been* dead all this time."

"Poppy." One word out of her mother's mouth, loaded with anguish. All this time, her mother had kept this truth from her, this fact that would have changed everything for her. *Everything.*

"How could you not tell me? How could you keep that from me? I don't even have the words. Please explain to me?" she demanded. "Only a horrible, selfish person would do that. You should have told me the minute it happened."

"Poppy...I... That time in our lives was horrible. When it happened, I thought telling you immediately would have been worse. I worried you couldn't handle it. I did what I thought was right and I'll always have that burden to carry—"

"What alternative could you even dream up to excuse this?"

"It wasn't like that."

"Keeping the fact that my father died over seventeen years ago from me wasn't like *what*? Horrible, disgusting, wrong?"

"Things happened when we left Graciella. There's so much you don't remember." Her mother's words rushed into the space between them, this new, unknown, horrible space of lies and mistrust and pain.

"What don't I remember?" Anguish flayed open her heart. Her chest physically hurt. It hurt to talk, to understand. She felt her face, wet with tears. All these years her dad had been dead, and she'd believed he hadn't wanted her, hoped that belief not to be true.

"The last time you saw your dad, you were so angry that you screamed at him, you..."

"Tell me. You owe me the truth. All of it."

There was a pause on the line. Her mother took a breath and Poppy thought she heard her mother choking back her emotion.

"You told him you wished he were dead."

"What?" The word felt ripped from her throat. A memory shoved itself into her emotions. She'd been crying then too, hitting her father's chest as he tried to hug her. As he tried to hug her goodbye.

"You were so angry at us, at him. Then we left, and you went completely silent for several days. You didn't sleep or eat or say anything. We made it to Boston and your dad was killed in an accident. I was in shock. You were in shock from leaving. You loved your dad so much, and I thought you would break if I told you. I thought you'd think it was your fault...after...what you had said to him."

The words stretched between them, and the child inside her was thrashing around wildly, a wounded animal crying out. *No. No.*

"We got you into therapy and you were doing so well, and you...you never asked about him. I knew that wasn't healthy either, but I...made a mistake. So many mistakes, and I wanted you to be healthy. And when I finally —"

"All this time I thought he didn't want me," Poppy interrupted her mother. Tears spilled over with the searing ache. "All these years..."

"He wanted you. He loved you. Even with all his shortcomings, he adored you. I had no idea you thought that. I misunderstood so much. I thought you were quiet because it was so personal for you. And you were still so silently angry at me for taking you away from Graciella. But you grew up and did so well at school, with art. But Poppy—"

"That's because I was afraid if I did anything wrong, *you* wouldn't want me either." It was hard to speak through the tears as her heart broke open in anguish and sadness and grief and every new way she'd have to examine things now.

"Oh no, love." Her mother was crying openly now. "I always wanted you. I always will. Your father and I both thought you were the best thing that ever happened to us. You *are* the best thing that ever happened to me. And Will adores you. I never meant to cause you so much pain."

Poppy held the phone to her chest. She was so cold, and she needed to sleep, to rest. "I'm...I don't know what to say. I...I need to go."

"Please don't, honey. There's more I—"

"I can't talk anymore right now. This is so much. I can't believe...all this and...I'm too exhausted."

"Do you have people with you?"

"Yes," she lied. "I'll call you...uhm, maybe tomorrow."

"I love you."

It was the last thing she heard before she ended the call. How could a person be numb and in pain at the same time? She wasn't present in her own body, except for the jagged edge lancing through her bones over and over again. She didn't have any people around. She never did. She was alone again. Always. The last words she'd said to her dad were that she hoped he died. *How do I live with that?*

Chapter Eleven

Restless and worried, Rafe combed his workshop for something to take his mind off his concern for Poppy. He'd left her, or she'd pushed him away, or both. He didn't quite understand what had happened. There was a pulse between them, and that kiss last night, even walking beside her this morning across the peaceful farm, he'd felt the click, like breathing for the first time.

Now, something was wrong. He'd seen it the minute she approached them outside the cottage. Her face had had the same shocked expression as yesterday after the phone call with her mom, when she'd relived her terror in France. *Worse.* And she'd been robotic. A forced smile barely stretched across her mouth. Stark freckles against too-pale skin, holding herself tight. But it was the haunted look in her eyes that made the biggest impact. A ghost had come and gone, taking with it the life from her soul.

He'd wanted to ask her what had happened, but he'd frozen again, tangled in his worry and fear. She'd been so quiet, so brittle, like she'd have broken into a thousand pieces if she'd had to speak. And he wasn't good at guessing what people needed or wanted. So he'd walked away, angry. Angry at himself for not knowing the best thing to do to help her, because he sensed she needed help. And maybe she couldn't ask for it. *Stupid, stupid man.*

He took all the raw pieces of wood out of the sideways shelves he'd built and tried reorganizing them, a task that normally calmed his mind, with the feel and smell of wood surrounding him. The labor worked his muscles and allowed him to focus on that as opposed to what his mind had trouble processing, but it wasn't working this evening.

When he paused and realized he hadn't even turned the heat on and his hands were brittle and freezing, he knew it was time to quit and go inside. Standing in the place he usually felt most comfortable, Rafe nearly choked on the worry churning in his gut.

Opening the large door had him bracing. Darkness had fallen and angry swirls of snow fought a fierce battle outside. Worlds away from the quiet, peaceful white landscape of this morning. Head bowed against the bitter wind and snow, he made his way in the dark to his house. When he dared to send a quick gaze toward the cottage, he saw one light on in the bedroom. Lonely. *She'd* looked lonely when he'd left her. And Christ, he knew how to recognize lonely.

His house was dark but warm, and he rubbed his hands to get feeling back in them. He stared at the contents of his refrigerator, but his hunger was dampened by his piss-poor mood. Food had also been an escape, cooking a soothing activity for him, more than that. He'd learned to cook at a young age. Tired of sandwiches on stale bread, he'd longed for the salsas and homemade tortillas his neighbors made. The first time he'd tasted a warm tomatillo salsa they'd made with dried chilis, his mind had been blown.

Now nothing sounded good. Instead of heating a bowl of soup, he flung himself on the sofa and stretched out his tired legs. His entire body, his mind, his heart were all wiped out. So much had happened in the last week. So much he hadn't even had time to process before Poppy had even entered his life. His mom...his mom was gone. The painful breath caught at his stomach, the realization, the truth. She'd died before he'd even made it to the hospital in San Diego. There'd been no goodbyes, no *I love yous*, only death and regrets.

They hadn't been close, but she had been his mom, and now? Now there'd be no more chances to try to make things right. Grief rolled over him, tasting like acid in his mouth. But it wasn't a brand-new feeling. He'd been waiting his entire life for her to choose him, to be the kind of mother who put her son first over her cheating drunken ex-husband—heck, for her to be the kind of woman who chose *herself* first over her ex. Her death only cemented the stark truth. She was gone. And he was still always alone.

Then Poppy had flown into his life. Had it really only been a few days? He'd been flung from one world to another several times and the landing back here with Poppy had felt awkward, but, if he was being honest, good too. Amazing and confusing and...just so much. A few pieces of fabric still rested across the arm of the couch. He fingered the light green one, almost the color of her eyes. He'd forgotten to take her sewing machine over to the cottage. There it was, situated in his nook.

She'd lined up several spools of thread on the windowsill and her scissors rested beside her machine. Her gloves and hat sat on the kitchen counter. *Tiny pieces of her scattered around.*

Outside, the wind screamed, a wicked witch blustering around, crying against the windows. It was how his insides felt now, churning and upset. More snow fell in thick flakes. Growing up in San Diego, he'd never seen snow as a kid and now he loved it. The peace it often brought, at least for a time, the cold, the fun.

But tonight, exhaustion took over and he didn't have it in him to watch the snow, even with the Christmas lights his friends had strung for him. He poured his tired, achy body off the couch and dragged himself to bed. *Maybe a good night's sleep will help.* Maybe in the daylight he'd have enough courage to talk to Poppy. From having that connection with her, to now where he felt like it had been severed didn't sit right in his gut. And the biggest worry was that she wasn't okay. Something had happened to her.

Unfortunately, when he got upstairs, his room smelled of Poppy, that field of spring flowers. It lingered in the air, in his bathroom, had permeated the sheets of his bed. She was everywhere — in his shop, in his kitchen, in his bed. Truly none of that would have mattered because she was in his mind too, and his heart already.

So, he stayed awake in the dark thinking about her. When he closed his eyes and let sleep finally take him under, he dreamed of her, an Irish goddess flying across the sea searching for him, to find her beloved.

* * * *

An unnatural quiet woke him. Or natural, depending on how he looked at it. The power had gone off, so nothing inside the house murmured with electricity. Everything was dark and silent inside. Outside, the storm blustered and raged. *What time is it?* He glanced out of the window at the eerie storm, gray and white in the surrounding black. *A hundred black stallions racing into battle.* His wandering thoughts stopped short with one image—Poppy. She'd told him herself she didn't like the dark. Both nights she'd slept with the lamps on in his bedroom. His cellphone rang as he climbed out of bed. Two a.m.

"Javier?"

"Rafe, power's out. We're worried about Poppy. The storm is too bad to drive in. Can you check on her for us?"

"I'm going now." He rushed the words into the space without a stutter, pulling his jeans and socks on as he spoke.

"Good." Javier sighed. "She needs someone to take care of her."

"I've got her," Rafe said.

"Thank you, son. Good man."

He tugged on his shirt as he raced down the stairs, threw on his boots and jacket and grabbed his headlamp and a flashlight from the kitchen drawer. And when he opened the back door, he was faced with a near whiteout, made so much worse at nighttime. Snow poured from the clouds while the wind whipped it into a frenzy. He leaned his body into the storm and made his way as fast as he could to the cottage.

All the lights were off. *Shit!* At least the door wasn't locked. He paused for a moment, contemplating whether or not he should enter her place without asking, but his worry over the dark scaring her won out.

"Poppy? It's m-m-me. Rafe."

Even in her dreams she was frozen. *Poppy.* Someone spoke to her in her dreams too. *How weird.* Her entire body was one big ache, similar to when the heat hadn't worked in Paris and she'd dressed in layers and bundled under all her heavy blankets. It was amazing how tired being freezing could make a person. And how much pain it could cause. Exhaustion and cramped limbs battled with each other. Even her bones hurt. Poppy opened her eyes on a scream as the darkness surrounded her. *Not dreaming, not dreaming. I'm certain I left the light on.* Fear kicked her pulse into a frenzy.

"Poppy? Are-are-are you okay?"

"Rafe," she called out, but her throat was exhausted from crying and the words felt like dust. "Rafe." She tried again to make it louder. Hopefully if he could hear her, he could find her in the darkness.

A bright light flashed in front of her face and she shielded her eyes from it.

"It's me." Rafe was there, a silhouette in the doorway.

"I'm c-c-cold." Now she was the one stuttering.

"Lost power. I can take you to m-m-my house. Make a fire."

Poppy swallowed the tears this time and nodded, then realized he might not be able to see her, and he definitely wouldn't be able to read her mind. "Yes," she said.

"Here." He handed her a flashlight. "Be right back."

When he returned, he had her coat and boots. She'd fallen asleep in her clothes. The power must have been out for ages, and she'd slept right through it.

Her coat wasn't too difficult, but her hands were shaking so badly she couldn't put her boots on.

"Here," he said again. He sat beside her on the bed and gently but quickly worked her feet into her boots while she huddled into her jacket. "Ready?"

"I'm so cold."

"T-trust me?"

He'd flipped the lamp on his head upward so she could look at him without being blinded. A serious but gentle expression shimmered in his eyes.

She nodded. She did trust him—his kindness, his intentions, his words, his warmth. Even after she'd shut him out earlier, he wanted to help her, *was* helping her. When he swept her into his arms and cradled her to him, she was too frozen to do anything but burrow into his chest as he carried her through the bitter snowstorm, fighting against the raging horrible wind.

Inside his house he carried her straight upstairs, set her on the bed and took her boots off. "Climb in," he said.

When he started to turn away, she gripped his jacket. "Please don't go. Can you, can you stay with me? You're so warm and I'm so c-cold…for so long." She was babbling, she could tell, but it wasn't lies. It was more truth than she'd told anyone in ages.

"Just starting a fire."

His words were rushed, trying to reassure her. Sometimes he had a hard time getting the words out. She didn't mind at all. She only wondered why it was easier for him on some occasions versus others. He stooped, lit the firewood in his bedroom fireplace.

Shrugging off his jacket and his boots, his body was a gorgeous dark shape in front of the glow of the flames as the red and orange swirls gained strength. They highlighted the strength of his body and his vulnerability. He was such a gorgeous man.

When he got the fire going, he said, "Right back."

Then she could hear him downstairs, closing the door and moving around. He raced back to her. It was another image that met with the fire to heat her, the thought of him quickening his pace to get to her. She snuggled under the covers and watched him. He took off his flannel and jeans, leaving only long underwear on.

"Better?"

She nodded then said, "Yes," when she remembered he might not be able to see her. Then she threw back the covers. "Quick, before the heat gets out." He seemed to need her nudges and that was fine with her, giving him the okay that she wanted to be with him. Wanted his touch, his words, his presence.

She'd been so exhausted, more mentally than anything. Then the cold had set into her bones, but now her limbs warmed and images of Rafe filled her space. Even in the dark, with him, she was no longer afraid. She certainly hadn't been afraid when he'd kissed her, when she'd kissed him. They'd made their own fire in his workshop, flames licking and climbing. The man had said a lot with that kiss. And his massive hands on her body, holding her to him, like he wanted to wrap his entire body around hers and make her belong to him.

Maybe she should let him speak more that way, with his body. She lost her thoughts when he climbed in, dragged the covers over both of them and pulled her to him as if it was the most natural thing in the world.

"Oh." She sighed into him and rested her head against his chest. "This feels so nice." He tangled their legs together and her body began to warm as if she'd been wrapped in the comfiest blanket ever. Finally, the aches from the cold began to leave her body.

"Cold feet," he said. His were furnaces next to hers. She rubbed her feet against his, seeking his warmth.

"Yours aren't. Thank you, Rafe, for coming to get me."

In response, his arms tightened for the briefest second around her.

"I...I'm afraid of the dark. Ever since...well...ever since what happened in Paris. Those nights I slept with the lights on. I've kept them on here too, but this is okays, with you. I mean, I'm not afraid with you."

"Good," he whispered against her head.

"Not just that." She wanted to clarify. "I like being with you."

"Hm."

"I *really* enjoy it," she whispered.

He didn't say anything out loud, but he'd started kneading her shoulder.

"Do you?" She paused. "Like it? I mean being with me?"

His swallow was audible and he stilled.

"Yes," he whispered.

And if she'd had any energy at all she'd have danced and twirled, maybe written hearts around his name in her notebook as if she were in high school.

"Are we...do you think we could do more kissing?" she whispered.

He braced again but didn't pull away. Gently he tipped up her head. She could barely make out the features on his face. And what he said wasn't expected at all.

"Can't see your eyes."

"What?"

"You...ear-earlier, you were upset?"

He'd noticed, and she'd shut the door in his face when what she'd wanted to do was fling herself into his strong, capable, talented arms and cry her eyes out.

"Very. I'm sorry." The apology came naturally.

"No. No apology. I...I can't see if you're okay now. For kissing."

Oh. *Oh.* How had she stumbled upon such a gentleman? Poppy untangled her arms and wrapped them around him, bringing their hearts flush against each other. Maybe their hearts could speak for them tonight.

His body relaxed, and he began rubbing her back in slow heated circles. And that felt delicious, amazing. The temperature in the room began to rise as the fire grew in strength and that, along with his soothing caress, brought her exhaustion settling in. Only it didn't feel horrible like when she'd climbed into bed tonight alone after learning the awful truth about her dad. It felt safe. More than safe—protected, cared for.

Her large yawn had him chuckling. *Oh sweet, sweet man with a sexy laugh.* He started to pull away. "I can sleep downstairs."

She didn't let him untangle them. "Can you stay?" She yawned again into his body. "I promise to be good. I'll behave."

Rafe felt her slip away into sleep, even with her body still holding on to his. But it was a while before he followed. Her words rang through his blood. *"I promise to be good."* What did that mean? She was a good person. He could tell that about her from only knowing her a short while. She was also good at talking, at eating, at laughing. At crying. He'd seen the leftover tear stains on her cheeks and her red eyes when the flashlight had highlighted her face. But he felt like she meant something else now. And it had him wanting to kiss her. He hadn't wanted to stop the other night.

"I promise to be good." Did that mean she was tempted to be other than good? Maybe he wanted her to be. No maybe about it. What would Poppy O'Brien of the wild red curls and adorable unfocused eyes without her glasses be like when she wasn't behaving?

She moved in her sleep. He noticed that with a vengeance now too. Her body wiggling against his, burrowing in, finding the right spot. A soft sigh came from her parted lips. *Hell! This is torture.* He wanted to trace those lips of hers with his fingers, with his lips, even with his tongue. He still had the taste of her in his memory from last night. *Hot cider and sugared donuts.* Would she taste different every time? Or was there a part of her true essence he'd tasted too? One he might recognize as her if he sampled again.

No, Rafe didn't slip easily into oblivion. He lay awake for a long time, listening to the occasional sound of the firewood popping and the wind swirling and her little sighs. He stroked his fingers through her long, soft hair and imagined a Poppy who didn't behave, and how they could misbehave together.

It was pure torture.

Chapter Twelve

Being warm feels amazing. Poppy stirred and snuggled under the blankets again relishing the heat. *Maybe I'm dreaming? No, it feels too real.* Especially her elbow, which was at an odd angle. Besides, her dreams of late had been bleak—Paris nightmares chasing her into sleep. No, right now she was definitely cozy, in a bed, in real life. When she opened her eyes and saw the fire glowing, she confirmed she wasn't dreaming of being warm. She actually was. And she was also snuggled against a deliciously ripped, warm-blooded male.

Oh. My. God. Rafe. She nearly squealed. He was asleep on his back, one arm over his head, the other under her with one of his amazing hands on her hip. She was plastered, her front to his side, her one gangly arm that had woken her tucked oddly under her body. But her other arm was currently on him. And somehow in the night she'd slipped her hand under the layer of clothing he wore to the bare skin of his chest. *Holy wow!*

Slowly, she focused on her senses. His chest rose and fell with his breath, and his heartbeat hummed under her fingertips. Breathing in, she was met with the scent of laundry soap and Rafe's body.

Pale light bathed the room from the windows beside the bed. *Morning, perhaps.* The covers were disheveled and cast off him. She blinked and tried to focus. *Is he wearing long johns?* She dragged her unfocused gaze down his body. She'd have to reassess her entire history of silly thoughts on long johns. There was absolutely nothing ridiculous about these ones, on him.

Good Lord, maybe she was dreaming. A vivid, intense sexy dream. She hadn't had sex in so long that maybe her subconscious was trying to tell her something. The long johns in question were open to his waist, giving her a glimpse of his skin. Below that they were still buttoned, but the cloth did nothing to hide any of his muscles. *Any,* including the bulge below his waist.

Poppy's skin bloomed with heat. Maybe it was her fuzzy vision exaggerating the…uhm…situation. She closed her eyes and opened them again. Maybe nothing was being exaggerated. What she knew for certain was that she wanted to stay right here, hot and tucked in and…and seriously turned on.

Poppy closed her eyes and breathed him in, trying to carefully snuggle closer, but as she came more awake, the awkwardness started to creep in as well. She hadn't even asked him if it was okay to touch him. Maybe she should move her hand away, but she didn't want to wake him either. He'd come for her in the dark, when she'd been scared and frozen to her bones. Without hesitation he'd saved her.

All right, maybe she was a bit dramatic, but to her it had felt like being rescued. He'd carried her through the blizzard, heated her up, kept her company, kept her safe. Her heart swooned at all that he'd done, and how he'd simply taken care of her so she could sleep, without taking advantage of her at all. She absolutely could not reciprocate by exploring his skin, warm and glorious though it was. *Soft surface covering hard muscles.*

Taking the quietest deep inhale she could, and cementing this experience to memory before it turned to dust before her eyes, Poppy counted to three in her head *one, two, three,* and, inch by inch, dragged her hand away without waking him. She was nearly to the edge of fabric, right in the middle of his stomach when his large hand came over his head, captured her hand and held it to his chest before she could escape.

"Eek." She did give a tiny squeal then and clenched her body to his. "Uhm, hi?"

"Mm." His rumbly voice sent delicious shivers through her, flinging her turned-on meter to outer space. Slowly, so slowly, he moved her hand across his skin, languorously, his eyes still closed, like he was learning her caress.

She let out a breath and enjoyed the journey, lost in the sensations of simple but oh so erotic connection. Letting him lead her hand over his stomach, up his chest to his breastbone, softly, to one pec where he tangled her fingers into his and grazed them over his flat nipple.

He gave a nearly imperceptible growl, then moved her hand to his other side, repeating the delicious sensations, and she was shivering again. But not from the cold. Her body heated all over with arousal. She was nearly panting.

"Poppy?" he whispered, sending his deep, sleepy voice into the moment.

"Rafe," she whispered back, his name the answer to every question.

He brought her fingers up, played with them, each one getting focused attention. *Yes, do that, do more of that. I never in a million years knew fingers were full of so many sensations.* When he brought them to his mouth and kissed her hand, she felt that kiss all the way to her toes, and, uhm, to other parts of her body. Wondrous aching parts currently pressed against his extremely muscled thigh. She nudged her leg against his ever so slightly, her need not slight at all.

Like the giant he was, with one swoop he lifted her and placed her on top of his body. *Oh my God!* She was going to hyperventilate. His heat, his muscles, his hard cock all fit against her so perfectly that she whimpered with relief at being this close, and with desperation to feel even more. He let her wandering fingers go and palmed her hips, holding her to him with attentive hands. "Okay?" he asked.

With her face against his chest and her heart racing, she answered, "Yes," and placed a tentative kiss on his bare skin close to his neck. He moaned and tugged her tighter to him.

"Again," he pleaded, or commanded. She couldn't tell. Her body responded by pressing into him and kissing him again in the hollow of his throat, against his rapid pulse. She was brave then, leaving her lips there and taking one tiny lick of his burning pulse, which was fluttering as fast as hers.

When he grunted and lifted her up his body, her libido danced in delight. He cradled the back of her head and brought it to his. Again, with the most reverent pace, he traced her lips with his thumb. Their mouths were aligned, hers hovering a mere sliver above his, his breath mingling with her panting and her small whimpers, the intensity of her need mixed with wonder and anticipation.

She'd never longed for a kiss so desperately in her life, and also, the waiting, *whew!* Plastered against such an amazing body, hers tingled so rapidly in response like all it would take was one more instance of him tugging against her bottom lip, one more rasp of her pelvis over his erection and she might come. It was intoxicating, making her feel as if she'd taken flight, her pulse, her body, her core, fluttering, waiting.

She couldn't help it. She moved against him, feeling absolutely everything as his hard cock rubbed against her pussy. Even through the layers of clothing, electricity sparked in her, starting right there between her thighs and shooting through her entire system. He moaned then and gripped her butt tightly with one hand to hold her steady or help her repeat the movement—it didn't matter because then he was kissing her. Kissing her with every ounce of his energy. Holding nothing back, he devoured her lips, tasting her with his tongue.

She opened for him and gave his tongue entry to swoop in and tangle with hers. *Holy wow!* She slid against him, aching for more.

He slid one hand around her head and held her there while he savored her mouth. Then he used his magnificent hands to caress her scalp, tugging her head back so he could explore her neck with his lips. When he moved his other hand from her butt, she wanted to cry out from the loss. But he was quick with his intention, pulling down her pajama top till it rested right above her breasts. The world stopped. His hooded gaze met hers briefly, then he swept his fingers over her skin, dipping them under the fabric to find her hard nipple.

She didn't know which turned her on more, the sweep of his featherlight touch, or how he concentrated on her reaction. God, she ached for more. It was amazing to rub against him, but it wasn't enough. Could he hear her begging? He pulled her top away, exposing one breast. Reverently, he held it and settled his mouth there.

"Yes," she cried out then, arching to help him possess her breast. Anything to help him. The angle nudged his cock right between her thighs, pushing the fabric of her bottoms into her pussy. The friction was incredible.

When she whimpered, he dragged his lips back to her mouth, capturing her sounds. Then with that intense focus of his, he swept her top completely off and over her head. He dragged her farther up, palming and sucking at her breasts, her tight, hard nipples. She mourned the loss of his cock right there against her wet folds, the place she wanted him this instant.

It was like he could read her mind. He stopped adoring her breasts, gripped her around the waist and dragged her body down his again, fitting himself to her. "Here?" he asked.

"Mm-hm." She darted her tongue out to taste his neck again, to feel his rapid pulse spinning. "Oh," she whimpered again as he hit the perfect spot. "More, please."

And he did, taking charge and moving her body. He could probably do anything with her body right this moment, so enraptured and turned on was she by his scent, by the feel of his hands on her, his hard glorious body underneath hers, silently whispering secrets and mysteries and teaching her how explosive they could feel together.

He held her still for a moment, held her on him and thrust along her seam, and she lost every sense of rational thought and came long and hard, splintering into a million wonderful floating pieces. And he captured her mouth, drinking down her moans and exquisite delight, perhaps as desperate to be connected to her as she was to him.

She went boneless on top of him, holding his head to hers. Holding him there in this most amazing space of intimacy she'd ever been in. He wrapped his arms around her, the steady strength of him cocooning her in the aftermath of such a delicious lighting storm.

"Wow," she whispered and dared to open her eyes. He was watching her still, his eyes dark and heated. *Wow,* she thought again. "That was…incredible." Each word she spoke moved her body against his still-hard erection. Every nerve in her body was lit up and when he pulsed against her, he teased more shivers of lust from her.

"You good?"

Gah, the man was still hard as a rock—he hadn't come—and yet every step of the way he'd checked to make sure she was okay. That was a heady feeling and one she'd never experienced with another lover. She wanted to bathe in this feeling, in the way he held her, studied her. It was need, pure and simple, pulsing through her. And she wanted to return all the sensations he'd given her. She stroked his cheek and snuggled deeper into him.

Silence cocooned them. She was just about to speak when the doorbell rang.

"Rafe," voices called from the front porch.

He let out a deep sigh, squeezed her tightly once then lifted her off him, placing her on the bed and throwing the covers over her. He handed her her shirt and gently placed her glasses on her face.

I'm going to melt into a puddle right here. She'd just had the most amazing orgasm ever. But stupendous orgasm *and* sweet considerate man? It was too much.

He stood quickly and dragged his jeans on and although Poppy was stunned out of her pure bliss by the interruption, she did get a clear view at his long johns before he dressed and left the room. Indeed, she had a new wild appreciation for long johns. And for a moment, she buried her head under the covers and squealed.

The voices from downstairs tugged her out from under her cave of fantasies. *I mean, whoever designed those long johns should be given a medal. Forget dresses and women's clothing, there absolutely need to be more long johns designers in the world. And the buttons, open like that, exposing his chest. All the parts that were still covered? Oh my!*

"Poppy?" Okay so maybe she was still lost in fantasyland. It was such a delicious place to be. She opened her eyes and peeked at Rafe. Hands on his waist, he pinned her with his eyes. His gaze raked over where her body was under the covers, with a scowl. No, not a scowl—heated, unquenched desire. Oh, her sexy lover was grumpy. Instantly she was turned on again. Would he climb back under the covers with her and get naked? Because as hot as those long johns were, she really, *really* wanted to see what he had underneath. *See, feel, kiss.*

"Katie and Cass and..." He gestured toward the door. "They need you."

"Me?" She blinked in surprise. Hm, she was conflicted. She really wanted to stay right here in bed with Rafe.

"A dress disaster," he said and stomped to the bathroom.

He flipped on the light. *The power's on.* But the house was still chilly. Reluctantly, she climbed out of bed and pulled on her large winter jacket. Rafe came back and sat beside her on the bed. He handed her a toothbrush and a pair of his wool socks. Then he took her hand, and even though he was looking at her fingers and not her eyes, she could feel the intensity of his gaze on her person, a laser burning into her. His profile was as handsome and solid as she'd ever seen. But his smile hadn't returned, or even his calm resting face. *Is he mad? Regretful? Oh no. Please don't let that be regret.*

"I'm sorry," she whispered and gave his hand a squeeze.

He startled and caught her gaze, full-on scowl in place. "Why?"

"I...uhm..." *Wow,* his eyes said so much. What exactly? Why was this so complicated for her? "For... well, you didn't get to, I mean, uhm." Embarrassed, she ducked her head into his neck. Even with his face frozen in granite, his body felt safe, lovely. Oh and he smelled so damn good. "You didn't get to come." His body tensed.

"That's not... I..."

His gentle caress on her fingers made her heart flip over. Then he brought her hand to his mouth and kissed her palm. "I'm the one who's sorry. Only, I-I'm not sure whether to be sorry I touched you, or so-so-sorry I can't climb back in bed with you," he said.

Then he walked out, leaving her alone in her puddle of lust.

Chapter Thirteen

Rafe tried to control the fact this his entire body vibrated with awareness of Poppy as he made coffee. He shouldn't have touched her like that. But she'd been draped over him, her hand tucked into him, her breath fluttering across his bare skin. Christ, her warm hand on his chest, so softly exploring him. There was no good excuse for touching a woman without permission, but he'd asked, hadn't he? His brain was short-circuiting. And she'd answered. There had been communication. Even through the haze in his mind he remembered their words, panted and whispered against each other.

No, the problem wasn't that he hadn't gotten permission. The issue was that she was his friends' cousin. The people who meant more to him in the world than, well, than anyone now. Was it a dishonor to their friendship? More than that, she was Poppy, the woman who paved a way with light following her. The woman who would singe a line through his heart before she left him in ashes.

"Thank you for taking care of Poppy." Katie set her gloves on the island countertop, closing the lid on his out-of-control thoughts.

"Of course." He tried to calm his brusque voice. Of course he would take care of her. They hadn't even had to ask him. He would do anything for her.

"We could barely see our hands in front of our faces during the storm, and it was a relief to know you were both okay. That you had each other."

Those last words were harder for him to swallow. *Each other.* Not many people in his life had ever been worried whether someone 'had' him. He was afraid to even imagine such a thing. He didn't answer. There was no sense in it.

"Yes," Cass said. "Did you weather the storm all right? Good idea putting two fireplaces in. I'm so glad we decided to do that at our house too."

"S-sure," he replied. He hadn't weathered anything well. He still burned for Poppy, even after the small taste of her. *Best not say that either.* There was a good reason he mostly remained quiet. Many good reasons.

Poppy flew down the stairs, setting the room alight with the scent of her, the whole being of her. "Hello." She gave Katie, Cass and Naomi hugs, fitting in, feeling comfortable no matter how long she'd been gone from this place or how recently she'd met some of these people.

He'd been here for years, and he still felt outside of it all unless he was working.

"Getting ready for the big day?" Her excitement was contagious. Everyone smiled, even him, caught in her shimmer. She played with a wispy silver scarf, weaving it through her fingers.

"Poppy, we need your help." Cass grimaced.

"My dress doesn't fit," Naomi blurted out. "It fit last month but I've grown or expanded or gah, I don't know, but it's too small and it's so damn beautiful and I want to wear this dress. It makes me feel special and it sparkles. It's…it's me. Only it isn't quite at the moment because I can't get it fastened. Oh shit!"

Cass' friend Naomi was a bucket of emotions. She unzipped the clothes carrier and gently, like it was made of real gold, unwrapped her wedding dress and draped it over the back of the couch.

"Wow," Poppy exclaimed, her smile wider and brighter than the sun.

His chest hurt looking at her, but he couldn't move his gaze away. He didn't want to. He'd never want to.

"It's so gorgeous! Who made it? May I?" she asked before she touched the fabric.

Naomi nodded. "A small designer in San Francisco. She's new and not well-known, but she made dresses for a friend of mine, and they were amazing. So she designed and made this for me. I knew I should have kidnapped her and brought her along for the week in case this happened."

"Okay, if it's well made, there should be a little seam allowance on each side for me to work with. If there's not, we'll figure out plan B, okay?"

"Okay." Naomi threw herself into Poppy's arms, tears streaming down her face. "Thank you."

"You should really thank Rafe. My machine got injured on the flight here and he fixed it for me with his magic I-can-fix-everything ability."

Was she teasing him or seducing him? Poppy glowed at him from across the room. Her eyes still held the haze of their kisses, of her orgasm. Her cheeks flushed right there in front of him. It was like her body communicated with his, both their wants and needs, their desires flowing between them. Not for the first time, Rafe cursed having visitors. But now it was because he wanted to go right back to bed and see if he could make Poppy's skin glow all over. Ashes be damned. He'd deal with his fire-damaged heart after she was gone.

* * * *

Joke was on him, wishing he'd had more alone time with Poppy that morning, because the fates warred against him. The women swooped her away. He got corralled into helping plow the roads and lanes of snow for the wedding guests who'd be arriving tomorrow, and any last-minute areas that needed his help. The first big wedding at Brockman Farms, aside from family weddings, with the storm of the century and so all hands were needed on deck.

It was cold but clear, with an intense blue sky and a few clouds. The work did him good, braced his thoughts, his emotions. The hard labor of shoveling snow worked his body in a way that brought some relief from the pent-up craving to have Poppy naked, under him, on him, curled into him. He huffed out a breath as the images sang through his mind. Yes, the labor was good. It was exactly what he needed to not lose his mind completely with thoughts of staying in bed all day with the beautiful siren who'd stolen his common sense.

As hard as he worked, he couldn't completely banish her from his mind, nor did he want to. When he returned to shower before dinner, her silver scarf sat on his kitchen counter, abandoned or forgotten. Rafe fingered the soft material. Her box of sewing stuff rested under the table in the nook, threads and fabrics spilling over the edges. And her scent lingered in every fiber of the house. It was a heady sensation, making him wish for more, for this to be his daily experience, a new normal, with her, the way she colored in his world.

The early winter darkness made the day feel shorter than normal too and before he knew it, the stragglers who weren't part of the rehearsal dinner had all gathered at the main house for a huge meal of burgers and fries. The constant hum of voices and laughter allowed him to stay quiet and observe, but even then, he had to be careful not to follow Poppy's every move with his eyes. There was more than one moment where he'd had to ground himself in the busy kitchen and simply breathe.

Now he was driving Poppy home. *Driving Poppy home.* He'd better not get stuck on that phrase. There was meaning in the word *home*. Brockman Farms was the first place he'd felt home in decades. He'd built a life here, a house, friends, even if his was mostly a solitary existence. But it wasn't Poppy's home, really. And he'd best not get hung up on that. Plus, he should take her back to the guest cottage tonight since the power had returned.

"Rafe," Poppy called from the passenger seat. "You're so serious."

Rafe glanced her way in time to catch the largest yawn he'd ever seen. "Hm. Tired?"

"Exhausted. But so happy. Weddings and love and family and laughter. I...I've missed all that. And I got to sew beautiful things, Rafe, beautiful things. It felt so good. And what a dream to have a wedding on winter solstice—so much promise ahead of them. I love the idea of that."

He wasn't one bit tired. Being in her presence stirred his blood. Now he couldn't even remember what it was like before Poppy.

"I fixed her dress and it felt so amazing to do that." She reached across the seat and took his hand in hers. He wondered if she was even aware she did it. "I haven't...well, today I enjoyed my craft for the first time in forever." She twined her long, graceful fingers with his.

This sensation was new and fragile. *Belonging.* "Good." How was he expected to talk when she touched him softly, her gaze focused on their connection?

"Could I sleep with you again?" she asked, her yawn catching the last of her words in a mumble.

"Hm?"

Her body was curled facing him, her head resting against the seat, her eyes closed.

"I'm so sleepy and I don't like the dark. I like *you.*" She placed emphasis on the word you as if she were mad that the world didn't understand her yearning. Maybe she was dreaming already. Completely unflustered and uninhibited. "I like you." Her words softened and her grip on his fingers relaxed.

He parked his truck in his garage. She took a deep breath and gave a shudder when he nudged her cheek. She was out. Gold thread was tangled in her hair. Funny how it looked natural there. A magical goddess who spun magic and riches.

Rafe had no problem carrying her inside. He'd been working with heavy machinery and large animals his whole life. But he'd never enjoyed using his muscles to carry something so precious *in* his life. His arms felt right around her, holding her close. He set her gently on his bed and worked her coat and boots off, and she tipped over onto the pillow like a ragdoll. A tired, happy ragdoll with a smile on her face.

Even in her sleep she smiles.

Rafe used the bathroom to change into a T-shirt and long sweatpants so he wouldn't freak her out if she woke in bed with him and hadn't remembered that she'd asked.

Then he climbed in, wrapping his arm around her — to keep her warm, of course. Finally, all the pent-up frustration seeped out of his body. He ignored the future and what it would mean and breathed in her scent.

"I like you too, Poppy O'Brien," he whispered into her neck. "I more than like you."

Easy to talk when no one could hear him.

Chapter Fourteen

Rafe was holding on to his fantasies of Poppy when he walked into Brockman House the next evening for the wedding reception. The wedding itself had been intimate, special guests only, but they'd invited him to the dance and dinner after. It had been another day without Poppy as they'd both helped with last-minute wedding prep again since early this morning. When he'd finished clearing snow and making sure all the paths were salted, he'd spent hours in his shop, putting his muscles through punishing labor to try to tamp down his craving for her.

He'd mostly accomplished it again, as long as he stayed away from his own house. Once he'd stepped into his bedroom, her scent overpowered any mantra of calm and cool he'd worked himself into. A cold shower had helped, somewhat. Driving alone over to the main house under the clear starry night with his window open and the bracing air filling his lungs had helped more. Alone was a feeling he recognized and could gain control over...or, had been able to before Poppy arrived. What was it she'd said? *"So much promise ahead of them."* That idea had taken root in his bones, dug deep.

The ballroom glittered and sparkled under the fancy decorations. People laughed and spoke. A dressy band played music from their spot in the corner. He glanced to the side where the grand new staircase circled down, and his heart fucking stopped. He rubbed his chest, not able to soothe the pain at all. Lost in her, he blinked. *Is that really Poppy?* Glammed up in a shimmery gold dress that molded to her body. High heels had her inches taller than the other women. Her face sparkled too, gold eye shadow and dark lashes.

She smiled and he lost his breath. She'd straightened her hair and had it pulled back in a sleek ponytail. A rich woman from Paris, or so he imagined. An artist or the model she draped her clothes in. Stunning, ephemeral. She tossed her head and laughed at something someone had said, sending her beauty throughout the room.

"Oh, Rafe, we're so glad you made it." The bride and groom stood hand in hand, jarring his attention away from Poppy.

"Thanks for all your help this week."

Rafe couldn't remember the husband's name, but he shook his hand all the same.

"I need to talk to the band, love." The groom kissed his new bride like they were the only two in the room. Connected, together, even as he walked away from her, their love threaded between them.

"She's magical, isn't she?" Naomi said.

"Huh?"

"Poppy." Naomi nodded her head in Poppy's direction. "She saved the day by fixing my dream dress for me. Ahh." Naomi sighed and smiled at her new husband across the room. "I'm not sure what I would have done if it weren't for her. And look at the dress she made for herself."

Rafe couldn't stop staring. The fabric was familiar, but the last time he'd seen it, Poppy had been lovingly caressing it as she'd unpacked it from the box in his living room. "She did that?" The shock came through loud and clear in his voice.

Naomi laughed in response. "I know, right? She waved her wand and *voilà*! I'm telling you." Naomi patted his shoulder. "Magical," she said, before she trailed away.

And again he stood by himself, watching Poppy, who was surrounded by others.

You're always alone. And Christ's sake, he didn't want to be anymore. And that was when he turned and left. He stalked out of the side doors to the deck that had been cleared of snow. Heaters warmed the space and more sparkling lights draped along the edge of the handrail. Rafe wished for the pure cold air to shock him, calm the stuttering inside him. He didn't belong here amidst this fancy perfection. He wasn't meant for someone as amazing as Poppy, no matter all the wishing he'd done the past few days. He was just a man by himself, a man with no family and no dreams.

He gripped the railing and gazed off into the night. All the cottages and apple trees shimmered with lights. *A midnight land dusted with wizard sparks.* At the thought of magic, she was there by his side. His own fairy — imaginary, a wisp of a dream.

"Rafe?" Poppy slid her hand onto his and tugged his fingers off the ledge, pulling his mind away from the dark places it had slid to. She had power over him.

He blinked her into focus. It was her, but it wasn't. Or maybe one more side of her. He let his fingers slide into hers and gave them a squeeze.

"Hi," she said, whispering out the soft word.

Her face was full of such intensity it almost startled him. But her grip was strong, and her eyes spoke their own language. She took his other hand and placed both of his on her hips. With that permission, his hesitancy slipped right out of him like a breath of air held too tightly. Impulsively, he pulled her flush against him.

"Hm."

He felt her hum against his neck where she'd placed her lips. He fucking loved it when she did that. "I... don't recognize you," he said.

She pulled back a step but didn't let go. "It's still me. What do you think?" Her hushed voice drifted like beautiful cold snow across his skin. She twirled lightly in front of him.

He shook his head and slid his hand to her back and brought her against him. "You're...stunning," he whispered, feeling her body heat against his, the intake of her surprise against his chest, the way she molded into him.

"Dance with me?" she whispered and led him inside.

In the doorway she stopped, his hand clutched in hers. He studied her, his focus lasered in on the way her pulse beat lightly through the skin on her neck. He brushed his thumb over it and watched her eyelids flutter.

"Look."

Over their heads hung mistletoe. He only knew what it was because he'd been roped in to help hang the wedding decorations. Hadn't paid any attention to it at the time. Now the glittering spell of the night, of Poppy's presence swirled around them. He stepped into her, cupped her cheek and leaned in to place a gentle kiss on her lips.

"God," he whispered. His body vibrated with need.

"Mm-hm," she agreed. The smile she gave him was one he hadn't seen yet, full of mystery and desire. He was aiming to dive into her lips again when she pulled him fully into the room and onto the dance floor.

He tried to camouflage the small stumble he made, but he knew it was hopeless. *He* was hopeless around her. She made him feel klutzy and breathless. He wanted her.

Poppy wrapped her arms around his neck, and he worked his around her hips again, pulling her to him. She was taller in her heels and it brought them almost eye to eye. Good thing it was a slow song. He could get away with being a pining fool, lost for her. Two songs he'd give her. If he made it that long. Dancing with her wouldn't be enough.

Chapter Fifteen

"I've missed you. Does that sound weird, even though we've only known each other for a few days, Rafe?"

He shook his head. He felt the same familiarity sweep over him when she was near, the comfort, the electricity. She fit into a spot of his that had been empty for so long.

"Are you really sorry about the other morning?" she whispered.

Rafe paused in confusion.

"About touching me? You said you might be sorry that you had. It's been bugging me the last two days because I wasn't. Sorry, that is."

"No," he answered immediately. With her warm body pressed against him and that sparkling, earnest look on her face, it was impossible to lie. Not that he wanted to, but he was trying to be careful with her, considering the way every cell in his body hungered uncontrollably for her. "Not sorry."

"Oh." Her soft voice sang and she beamed her smile at him as all her uncertainty seemed to vanish. "If…if I asked you for something, would you give it to me?"

Her words flitted through his ear while they danced. So bold, staggering, like the models she probably dressed, but with soft curves. He loved her curves.

"Anything." Surrounded by people, many dancing, some eating hors d'oeuvres and drinking champagne, music and sparkly lights their background, Rafe had only one focus—her. The rest was a smudged canvas, inconsequential, unnecessary.

"I'm ready to go. I want you to take me to your bed."

The softest, but surest words he'd ever heard from her hammered through his body. Rafe stopped still, right there in the middle of the dance floor. The mummer moved around them out of focus. Before him was all he wanted. Bold and vulnerable, both at the same time. That's what she was, and it was a heady combination. It revved his blood even more.

"Now?" Why was he pausing? Why wasn't he grabbing her hand, tossing their coats on and racing her home in his truck immediately?

"Yes, Rafe," she insisted, huffing out a small laugh. Desperation flew between them. "If you want to, that is. Please."

It was the *please* and the way she gripped his neck when she said it, holding herself to him, like he was the only thing keeping her upright. It only took a second longer before he gripped her hand and led her through the foggy mess of people and music. Another burst of laughter bubbled out of her as he grabbed their coats and they both walked as fast as their fancy shoes would carry them to his truck.

He helped her up into the passenger seat and was around the hood and jumping in before she even got her coat on. Leaning across the seat, he had to kiss her, had to taste her in the chill of the night. It took all his strength to pull away and put the truck in gear. The ride might have been a blur, but the ice and snow made him slow down and concentrate. Poppy was precious. The thumping organ behind his ribs compelled him to take good care of her.

"Stay," he gently ordered when they arrived at his house. When he made his way to her door, she had her shoes in her hands and was giddy when he lifted her in his arms.

"It's so beautiful out tonight, isn't it?" Her voice was a feather against his neck. He shivered at the caress. "You're not cold, though," she whispered and held on to him, leaning in to place her lips against his throat, as he tried to climb the garage steps into the house without fumbling both of their bodies onto the floor.

"Neither are you."

"You know I can walk, right?" She nipped at his ear and wiggled into his embrace, not one bit dismayed, it seemed, that he was carrying her.

"I like y-y-you in my arms."

"So do I," she whispered and tightened her arms around him.

"When I carry you," he said, pausing in the hallway to lean against the wall. She'd left his small lamps on in the living room, and they cast a welcoming glow down the hall. Something familiar to comfort them. When before he'd always returned to the dark, lonely house. All these tiny fingerprints she was leaving on his home, on his life, on his heart. "I feel your warmth against me." It was remarkable how steady his words were. The stuttering was in full throttle in his chest, however.

"*You're* the warm one, a furnace lighting me up." She reached around and teased her fingers through his scalp.

He drew in a breath at the soft, insistent feel of her fingers on him. The sound of their voices anointed the near-dark magical feel. Her words raced through his body, grounding him, fueling him.

"In my arms, I can feel you here," he said and ran his hand along her thigh. "And here." His other hand, under her arm was barely steady as he stroked an invitation along the underside of her breast. He caught her small whimper with his mouth, and their kiss turned from steamy and seductive to overwhelmingly hot in an instant. She turned in his arms, grabbing his head with both hands and wrapping her legs around his waist. Somehow in the pleasure-induced haze, he adjusted his grip to cradle her ass and keep her against him. Her dress had slid up and he could roam his hands freely over her skin, the lace of her underwear.

She kissed him with a passion that lit his own. He couldn't get enough of her lips, tasting and sucking, breathing in her air, grinding her into him. They were heated breaths and lips and tongues racing, diving for each other, eating at each other. It was a good thing the wall propped them up, because he felt both powerful and boneless.

"Are we…" She panted and kissed him again. "Are we going to make it to your bed?" Awe sang through her words.

Her beauty and lust fogged his brain. Need, white-hot desperation, his body for hers, thundered in his bones. She ran her fingers over his cheek, and it was her soft caress that brought him an ounce of reality. Yes, they were making it to his bed. This time. Later, hopefully another time, they could be so lost they ripped each other's clothes off in the hallway and stumbled to the floor, but tonight it was too cold and he wanted her in his bed, now. He lifted her closer to steady her and headed for his goal. She tucked her head into his neck and laughed as he raced up the stairs.

"God, I feel so free and wild, Rafe. This night, the stars the romance, the dancing and love and ever-afters." She spoke against his skin, every word its own kiss. "You, this, us, together. I never knew it could be like this. That I could feel this much for another person."

She could be speaking for him. Her words echoed through him. He let her slide slowly down his body as he set her back on solid ground and switched on the bedside lamp, cocooning them in a glow. She untucked his shirt and stared intently at the buttons, undoing one, then another. He really thought his heart might beat out of his chest at that moment, at her face flushed with desire. No one had ever looked at him that way. It dragged his lonely soul out of its murky hiding place. When he shrugged out of his shirt and her palms met his chest, he felt that connection everywhere.

With shaking hands and before he did rip her clothes off, he turned her in his arms and carefully tugged down the zipper of her dress. He sucked in a slow breath as her skin appeared to him. He ran his fingers along each soft glimpse and felt her body arch toward his touch. When she spoke, he captured her whispered, "*Rafe*" and locked it away for safe keeping.

She reached around and undid her bra for him. Then, as if shy all of a sudden, slowly turned back toward him, her hands over her chest. "I'm...wow." She breathed out.

"Okay?" he asked and wrapped his arms around her, cradling her to him. He brushed his lips against hers.

"So okay... It's been a while since I've been naked in front of someone, and never in front of someone so beautiful."

"Huh?" He huffed. "I'm big and clunky."

She laughed and shook her head. "You're beautiful to me, Rafe. So, so amazing. Strong and hard and intense. Soft in here." She rested her hand over his heart.

"We can stop anytime. If you're uncomfortable," he whispered and ran his hands through her silky hair, memorizing her scent, the new musky perfume she'd dabbed on her skin.

"No." She smiled again and with the joy and unabashed-ness he'd been drawn to from the beginning she threw her arms around him. "Take me to bed, Rafe. Kiss me and touch me and do everything. I want this. I want to have sex with you. I want to explore this...all these feelings inside. They're going to burst out if you don't kiss me."

He took her mouth before she could utter another plea and her moan stripped the last flimsy thread of control he had. Dizzy with her scent and the taste of her, he lifted her and knelt with her on the bed, spreading her out beneath him.

Desire had never felt so heady, so all-consuming and free at the same time. Poppy thought she might fly. Perhaps she already was. Everywhere Rafe touched her, kissed her, whispered against her electrified skin made her blush, made her shiver, made her entire body hum with life, with things she couldn't even name. His large hands explored her body with fervor. And she writhed against him, following his touch, how hot his hands were. Grasping and kissing him where she could, his chin, his chest, the forearm he propped himself on beside her. He stroked her body, exploring with his fingers, with that extra serious gaze of his, as if he'd discovered a rare new creature in her. And she reveled in both his caresses and his perusal.

One moment of shyness had been wiped away by the open look of arousal in his eyes, and even then, his ability to say they didn't have to do anything, to put her feelings first. She felt his blood racing beneath her fingertips, and she knew this was exactly where she wanted to be.

He placed needy kisses along her belly, dragged his body up hers and palmed one of her breasts, flicking his thumb over the nipple. "Fucking gorgeous," he growled.

She shuddered. His dark eyes grew hooded, and he repeated the motion before he took her nipple into his mouth, kissing and sucking it as expertly as he'd done to her lips. Her body bucked in return, and she slid one of her legs around his body to anchor him to her.

"Seriously, are you an expert at this or what?" Her words were short huffs of inquiry in between each tug of his lips. And she felt his own grunt in return against her skin which sent even more shivers of delight snaking through her body, shooting right to her core where she was so, so needy. He was so open and honest in his words, in his response to her. Rafe undone was a beautiful sight.

"Your body makes me needy," he said.

Yes, that! He read her mind. He dragged his lips across her chest and attacked her neck with his expert lips, nipping at her skin with his teeth while he let his hands wander over her body, fast then slow, rough and gentle, learning her. She wrapped her arms around him and explored the smooth taut planes of his back, so strong and powerful. Talk about powerful — his cock rubbed against her inner thighs in teasing motions she could sing about. It was all she could do to pant out her breaths.

Poppy took his head and brought their mouths together. "I think I could kiss you forever," she said and laved her tongue along his lower lip.

He was breathing heavily too. He changed the motion of his body as it rubbed against hers, slowing the pace, which heightened the sensations. He took over the kissing and devoured her mouth, rocking so slowly against her. Everything aroused her, the sheet against her skin, his fingers on her scalp, the small hairs on his chest razing against her tight, hard nipples, her breasts heavy with want, how hard he was. The kiss became frenzied, both her and Rafe diving and sucking. She dug in her heel and tried to rock her body closer to his, to rub her needy, needy pussy against his hard cock, to find relief. "Oh God!"

He rolled off and fumbled with the drawer on his bedside and she couldn't help it — she had to keep touching him. Being separated was not an option. She reached out and stroked his butt, big and glorious and leading to such strong thighs. God, he had a great butt. She arched her body and drifted her fingers over his soft skin, to his thighs, getting lost again in the sensations. Even her feet felt bereft apparently, as she teased his calves with her toes.

"Rafe," she panted. "Hurry."

When her fingers explored his side, he jerked and grabbed her hand. "No tickling," he reprimanded. And oh, he was so sexy, eyes dilated, voice gruff with need, a hint of command. He finished sliding on the condom and she stilled momentarily at the sight. When she reached out toward him, his hands clasped hers. He tangled their fingers together and dragged them over her head while he settled himself back right where he belonged, nestled between her thighs.

She wiggled under him, loving the friction of his rock-hard length grazing against her. How had she missed out on all these feelings before? Sex had never felt this good. And they were only in the caressing and kissing stage. *Oh!* And the tasting stage. She let out a huff as he licked down her belly. Letting her hands go, he tasted and savored until he was a breath away from her pussy and he paused. Paused and set all that enormous strong focus on her right there. She swore her heart beat from there now.

And he didn't make her wait long. He teased along her folds, gently but it felt…it felt massive. He dragged his nose and his tongue along her wet, pulsing skin. The scruff of his jaw, the shock of it surprised her and she bucked up toward him. The orgasm ripped right through her in electric rolls of movement and cries as she grasped onto the sheets.

Fucking hell, she made him feel like shouting to the world. Watching her body coil and spring and soar through her orgasm while he stroked her thighs and held on made him feel a million feet tall and joyous and in awe all at the same time. His body was primed to take her now, make her his, move with her. But he made himself pay attention to her pleasure.

When she quieted, her breaths still huffing out of her and she sang his name, "Rafe, wow. Come here. I need you." Only then did he climb up her body and nudge against her wet opening, pausing as he studied her eyes, glossy and shimmering with gold.

"Can I?" he asked, his own voice harsh, in awe over her beauty, over their shared intimacy, that she'd allow him to give her pleasure. It nearly overwhelmed him. How a thing so delicate and powerful at the same time, so beautiful and uncertain, so soft and surprising could want a thing like him. *Not things*, people, human beings. But his brain had short-circuited as soon as he'd stepped into the ballroom and seen her glittering under the lights, as if the magic was created solely for her.

"Oh yes, please, Rafe. I need to feel you inside me. What you do to me." Her voice was full of pleas, but her caress on his cheek was gentle, steady.

He listened to her then, captured her hand in a kiss and slowly notched himself into her. She gasped and her smile was lopsided, and he felt both in his dick, as she coiled again around him this time. *Jesus Christ.*

"Wow," she whispered with a soft huff. Rafe cradled her head in his hand and pushed, seating himself in her warmth. Her eyes simmered as he slowly pulled out and thrust back in. *This is the most intense moment of my life.* She wrapped her around him and dug her fingers into his butt, tugging him closer into her, matching his movements, matching his awe.

"Poppy." He struggled to get her name out, to breathe through the pleasure as it built in him.

"I know, Rafe," she whispered, holding him tightly this time.

She gave little cries, and he swallowed them with his mouth, devoured her lips, sucked on her tongue. Quickening his pace till he was pumping in fast reckless waves, he chased her power and her release. He gave one last push with all his strength and let his body come undone, as hers coiled once more and pulsed around him, rocking them both into oblivion.

Chapter Sixteen

Rafe washed his hands and returned to the bed. Poppy was on her stomach, her hand curled around a pillow, the blanket snaked haphazardly around her body.

"Oh, can we do that again and again and again?" Poppy's voice was cute but muffled by the pillow she'd shoved her face into. When she pulled her gorgeous head back out, her entire face was flushed and happy. Joy glittered all over her skin.

It was Rafe's turn to laugh. He swiped a finger over her lips, hoping to capture one iota of her essence. Even that single touch had him growing hard again. Her silky skin under his fingertips. *Her.* Christ, he wanted to bound down the stairs, fling open the door and shout his laughter, his own happiness to the world.

Her smile softened and she studied him. "Was it okay for you?"

She pulled the sheet up as a wave of something, uncertainty perhaps, came over her and he leaned in and kissed the words, the doubt, away. He twined his fingers in her hair and held her while he poured all the feelings wanting to burst out of him into her.

"Oh." She softened against him.

"Again. Yes, please," he whispered against her mouth and felt her smile return. "We can…we can stay here all night and the next." He gently tugged the sheet away and pulled their bodies flush together.

All worry gone from her expression, she snagged her arm around his neck and wrapped her body around his. "I'm not cold anymore," she whispered before she brought her mouth to his and kissed him again.

Me neither. I might never be cold again.

"Rafe?" She'd pulled away from their heated kiss, but her eyes were closed, her face, flush and open.

"Hm?" He kissed her chin, her eyebrows. God, he wanted to kiss every inch of her, memorize her so he could feel her in his cells.

She wigged her body against his, tentatively, slowly, and he paused his kissing to watch the expression on her face. She was lost in her pleasure, or maybe embracing it. Teasing his neck and his shoulder she arched into him, her pelvis right against his cock that was rock-hard for her, instantaneously.

"I…" Her mouth curved into an *oh*. She rubbed her wetness against his leg, moving sinuously so her pussy was angled right over his cock. She was spectacular and he had to hold himself still or he'd come right then and there all over her, all over the sheets. "I need you…" She stilled, her breath coming heavier. "Now," she whispered and brought her hand to the small of his back to hold him there while she slipped her warm heat along his shaft.

"Again. Please," she begged, writhing against him.

Now tunneled through his brain, his blood on fire. He felt around for the strip of condoms, had one open and on faster than he knew he was capable of without losing her embrace. She was so wet and hot for him he had to touch her. He stroked his thumb through her folds, swollen and ready for him. She whimpered and chased his hand with her body. *So eager and uninhibited.*

It had never been like this for him with a woman, where she was both so full of desire for him and so unafraid to show it, to move her body in a way that made her feel good. He wanted to take notes. He wanted to help her feel amazing. He stroked himself once, twice, until she brushed his hand away and took hold of him herself. Then she opened her eyes, met his gaze with hers. "You feel it too?"

He nodded. "Yes." He owed her more than nods. He owed her the words, the confirmation.

She wrapped her body around his and dragged herself closer to him. He was drugged by her show of pure arousal and need. She slid her body into place, just enough so the tip of his cock was at her entrance. She paused.

"Wow," she said again, and he *knew*, he agreed.

Yes, wow. He didn't want to interfere, but there was nothing that said he couldn't aid in her pleasure, and her soft, heavy breast was right there. He teased her nipple, watching her, always watching her. And he was rewarded with her moan and the way she bowed her body into him, giving him her breast to do what he wanted as she slowly urged her body around his cock.

"Fuck," he grunted out and buried his head in her chest, nipping her there, tasting her arousal on her skin, as her body clamped around him and she came in tight little grips around his dick while whimpering out her pleasure, her body shaking with the movement. The sexiest fucking thing he'd ever witnessed, ever shared with another human being. He wrapped his own arm around her then, holding her tightly to him.

Only when she was done did he seek his own release, moving in short, deep thrusts. So tight, she was so fucking perfect wrapped around him. He kissed her while the pressure built, moved his mouth to her shoulder, sucked at her skin and grunted out his own orgasm, all the while keeping her body anchored to his.

* * * *

Rafe woke hard as a rock. A sliver of the morning sun lit the sky. He lay on his back, comfortable, or as comfortable as he could be in this position. Poppy sprawled beside him on her stomach, one arm draped over his chest, one leg over his, with her knee cocked up. Her warm sex hugged his thigh, and he closed his eyes and envisioned sliding right inside her, bare, as the morning light made its way over the snowy farmland, in the quiet of his bedroom, with her sleepy and sexy and...and...everything he'd never even dreamed of, because he'd learned long ago not to dream.

His gaze zeroed in on her mouth, open with a soft and happy expression. Her burnished curls tangled around her head. He brushed the locks gently off her cheek, letting his fingers linger for a moment. She breathed deep and snuggled into her pillow, completely unaware of how hard he was for her, again.

She enjoyed her sleep. He'd noticed that. Or maybe the jet lag still clung to her. He smiled, remembering their night. After exhausting their bodies with each other, they'd taken a hot leisurely shower then stormed the kitchen for sustenance. Crackers and cheese and leftover banana bread had never made so delicious a meal. He suspected it was because of how starving and sated they were, but he wasn't complaining one bit.

Rafe quietly climbed out of bed, dressed and made his way through the gorgeous cold morning to his workshop. Something thrummed beneath his skin, something creative needing to come out. And since he couldn't use his creativity on Poppy this exact moment, he concentrated on an idea that had been percolating in his mind for the past few days.

Not oak, oak's too boring a wood for Poppy. Pine might work, but she's more intricate than that. Maybe…hm, black walnut could work. Rafe fingered through his racks of wood, letting his hand wander until he found the right piece for his idea. *Yes, black walnut. Rich, lustrous, textured, like Poppy.*

The ringing shop phone jarred him from his reverie. "Yup," he answered. "Sure thing, Adam." Rafe grabbed his jacket and hat and a pair of work gloves. *Nothing like fixing a snowplow in the middle of winter, outside.* He could fix any machine he'd ever encountered. Rafe grinned again. Nothing could wipe the smile off his face this morning. Of that he was certain.

* * * *

"Damned ornery piece of metal. Shit-for-brains rusty old menace."

Poppy froze where she stood in the kitchen and listened to Rafe swearing on the porch. She peeked through the window in time to see him chuck his boots and hang his jacket. She wanted to laugh at the string of swear words he'd expelled succinctly without one hitch whatsoever, and at the grumpy frown that preceded him into the kitchen. But she swallowed all thoughts of humor when he locked his focus onto her. Slowly his gaze gathered into one point of focus. Fire, darkness, intensity all swirled in his gaze.

Rafe slowly aimed his study down her body, burning a path along her skin. "What are you doing?" Each word was punctuated by a searing emotion.

Oh. Poppy took a step back. Her hand shook slightly so she set the French press on the counter. Rafe stepped forward, midnight hair, midnight eyes, banked energy taut in every muscle.

"Making breakfast?" she offered.

Rafe quickly glanced around the kitchen then right back to her. She hadn't really started yet. Eggs and coffee were all they had. But she'd wanted to make him something, even if cooking eggs kinda freaked her out. He'd left her another note by where she slept. And although she'd have to talk to him about that whole leaving-her-alone-in-bed situation, she adored the little notes he wrote, making sure she knew where he was, leaving her a cup of coffee or tea.

His gestures spoke of care and concern and...well, they were more than that to her, but it wasn't up to her when someone decided to love her or not. She'd learned that lesson many times. Still, there was a part of her that loved to pretend. Often, over the years, it was the pretend that had gotten her through one day to the next. *Do I want him to love me? So, so much.*

"Breakfast?"

"Well, uhm...I didn't get very far." Poppy took another step back, now stuck in the corner of the kitchen, pinned in place by his fierce, hooded expression. Was he...? He moved another step closer. "Are you angry?" She faltered. "At, uhm, me?"

He shook his head. One more step and he hovered in her space. Not one inch of her felt threatened as he crowded her, energy radiating off of his body. She gripped the counter. His hands fisted at his sides. One made a move toward her hip, then hesitated. His eyes were fire roaming over her. "You're dressed," he said, his voice harsh with need.

Oh. Oh. Poppy let out a breath. *Silly, tortured man.* She understood. "So are you," she accused playfully and feathered her hand down his chest.

"Had to work." There was not one hint of playfulness in his heavy words.

"Mm. I know."

"Got dis-distracted." He reached for the button on her pajama top, toying with it but not undoing it. His concentration on that spot was so intense she thought he might singe through the fabric with his desire alone. His voice had turned to a harsh whisper as he inched even closer.

"Huh." One simple word was all she could get out. She reached for his hand on her button.

"I'm cold," he insisted. His fingers were freezing. *Poor baby.* And she was on fire. It was a dazzling combination.

"I'll warm you." The thought that she could be the one to comfort him thrilled her, spun through her body, pooled low in her belly. Needy, she was so needy. As if they hadn't spent hours last night satisfying each other. As if she'd never ever been with a man before and had been waiting, for eons. She was all desire. She could barely breathe, and she craved his touch.

She undid the buttons herself, each one, slowly, reveling in the sparks that ignited in his eyes. Then she used his hand to part the top. His cold fingertips brushed against her stomach, along her ribs, until she pressed his hand against her breast. The chill had her drifting toward him and moaning. It felt so good against her overheated skin, the shocking contrast of it all. Rough chilly fingers against her hot body. So right, so electrifying.

Rafe had both hands on her skin then, parting her top and shoving it off her arms. Then he put his chilly hands down her pajama bottoms and gripped her butt, tugging her right against his hard body. "So warm." His voice was gravel against her neck as he leaned into her, and in another second had her bottoms shoved to the floor. He slid his hands right back up at a lightning pace and lifted her onto the counter.

"Oh." It was all she could get out at the cold surface against her bare bottom. Her entire body whimpered toward him, seeking contact. She needed him touching her. But watching him shrug off his jeans was almost as delicious. His body was a sight to behold, such large defined muscles. She grabbed onto his shoulders, ran her hands over his sexy long johns that did their job and kept his torso heated. He had buttons too and her hands shook as she undid them. He didn't touch her but watched her with that scorching thirst in his eyes.

When she reached the lowest button, she paused. *Oh my.* Poppy huffed out a sigh. Rafe had his arms out and let the long johns slide off, shrugging his boxers away with them. Never taking his gaze off her, he fisted his cock with one hand and smoothed the other to her lower back.

"God, Rafe." She wanted to put her hands on him, but when he slid his cock along her wet seam, she gripped the counter to hold on. He kissed her neck again while he played with her pussy, teasing her.

"Need you, *want* you," he said and snaked his tongue along her shoulder, sending erotic shivers down her arm. He brought their bodies flush and the feel of her hard, aching nipples against his skin was electric.

"Please, come inside me right now." Her words were demanding — they flew on a life of their own.

"Need a condom." He nipped at her earlobe.

"I-I..." She could barely talk. He was going to make her come naked on a counter with barely the tip of his cock brushing against her like some sweet hidden torture technique. "I'm safe. I..." She panted, trying to find a cent of rationality. "And it's been a long time since..." *Oh.* His body tensed around her.

"Me too. A *long* time. I-I've never been with someone bare."

Poppy laughed from pleasure, from need, from revelations, and threw her arms around him.

He grabbed her. "Upstairs. Bed."

She shook her head and bit at his neck. "I can't wait. Please, Rafe." Licking up his neck and kissing his jaw, she turned his head so their lips met. One hover of breath as their eyes locked for a second. Flames took over his beautiful dark irises. They lit with a spark of gold. Finally, Rafe reached between their bodies, fitting himself at her entrance again. *Yes.* Poppy helped, thrusting forward right as he drove inside her. *Finally.*

He grunted against her forehead, tightening his arms around her. Poppy crossed her legs behind him and held on as he powered into her. Urgency coiled tightly inside her. Her entire body shivered with the sensations, and she shook and whimpered against him, gripping him as hard as she could, as if she could climb inside him, as if it were life or death, beauty or darkness.

Close, she was so close. She wanted it, but she also wanted to make this feeling last and last and last, the burning ache between them, the grunting, the moans, the way she panted out his name, "Rafe, Rafe, Rafe."

Holding on to him, she reveled in his tight muscles beneath her fingers as he stilled, his cock swelling inside her and that was it. Her body exploded into fireworks around him, pulling him in deeper. Until he lost control too, lost himself in her, in the sensations that rolled through his powerful body into hers.

Entwined, they slumped against each other, both of them breathless and sweaty. She placed a gentle kiss against his skin. She couldn't find words. Even if she could have, she doubted she could have spoken them aloud.

"Never in my life... Poppy." He breathed the words against her quietly. At least one of them could form words right now.

"Mm-hm." She snuggled into his embrace. He didn't even need to finish his sentence, but she knew what he meant, or hoped. Because never in her life had she felt this way either, like their connection was too magnificent not to soar into the stars and sparkle. Even beyond the spectacular physical feelings. They were simply meant to fit together.

Belonging. The word was headier than any orgasm, even if it was the orgasm of a lifetime. Poppy giggled out her emotions, her nerves, her ridiculous flowy thoughts, and Rafe tugged her head back and swallowed her laughter and her joy with his kiss, soft and careful and oh so beautiful.

Chapter Seventeen

They were in the same booth as the first time, but today they sat snuggled next to each other. *We have a special booth!* Her brain was no less loopy, even after a shower and getting dressed and riding into town for pizza. The whole restaurant might have been just for them, for all that Poppy noticed anything else. More accurately, she noticed certain things acutely. The confident but soft timbre of Rafe's voice and how his throat moved when he spoke. *Holy goodness. Can a throat be sexy?* It sure was when he spoke, when she kissed along it and felt his breath hitch, when he swallowed his root beer.

Dang, she'd had to wipe away her drool from the sight of him drinking soda. *How ridiculous.* She wanted to stroke his neck, pet it, kiss it. Heat teased along her thigh from where their legs rubbed against each other. Which was nothing compared to how Rafe's soap became something bolder when it was on his body, clinging to his clothes. She had her arm looped around his and she kept leaning her head in to sniff his arm. And he grinned at her the entire time. She truly was ridiculous. And it felt wonderful.

"Hello, you two. Ready to order?" The same waitress from last week had a huge smile on her face looking from Poppy to Rafe.

"Yeah," Poppy said. She glanced at Rafe, who hadn't taken his eyes off her. "Same as last time?" she asked.

He nodded.

"Graciella Pizza and knots, please. Our usual," Poppy said with a huge smile.

"Coming up," Meg said and winked before she turned and headed toward the kitchen.

"I feel giddy," Poppy whispered, catching his eyes with hers. Rafe linked their fingers together.

"Yeah," he agreed.

"It feels really good," she whispered again. "I don't recognize this feeling."

He smiled and shook his head, smoothing his thumb along the back of her hand. Her stomach grumbled. "Always so hungry?" He raised his eyebrows and his mouth quirked as he teased her. *God, he's gorgeous when he teases me.*

"Starving," she said on a sigh.

Their pizza and garlic knots arrived, and they untangled from each other to devour their food, sharing smiles and secret touches under the table. It felt amazing to be so comfortable in someone else's presence. To talk if they were inspired to, but also to enjoy the silence with each other. Her body was light and warm, her smile constant. Even her worries were smoothed away.

After lunch, they strolled through the grocery store, filling a cart, holding hands. "Shall we go for a walk?"

she asked as they loaded the bags into his truck. The day was breathtaking, brilliant. Blue sky, crisp winter air, sunshine and holiday cheer decorating the town.

"Oh," Poppy said on a hush. She stopped abruptly and lost hold of Rafe's hand. He turned and came back to her. Her old house. Right here on Main Street. She'd shoved it out of her mind again, but not really. Here it sat in daylight, in the middle of all the cheer. Different from that first night she'd seen it. Now it was empty and lonely. Curtains no longer graced the front windows. All the decorations she'd seen last week had disappeared, as if they'd never been there in the first place.

"Poppy?" Rafe stood behind her and settled his hands on her shoulders. "Okay?"

"Mm." She nodded or shook her head, not sure which she meant, yes or no. It wasn't okay, but she didn't want to discuss it, not here, not now when the cold seeped back into her bones from all those long-ago memories. Not when she'd been so warm seconds ago with Rafe.

If she'd known seeing her old house would send ice over her bones, would she ever have returned to Graciella? She leaned against him, trying to soak up the heat from his body. "Let's go." She struggled to get the words out through the rock that was lodged in her throat. She took his hand and without another word, led him to his truck.

Poppy tried deep breathing on the ride. She kept hold of Rafe's hand, attempted to control the woozy feeling running through her body. Rafe kept glancing at her, but he didn't speak. And neither did she. She didn't have it in her to fill the empty space right now.

The empty space was its own voice clamoring in her head for attention.

They were quiet on their way into the house, but she sensed his eyes on her, his worry. Was that what true connection felt like? Being so entwined with someone they could feel each other's emotions? Even the difficult ones? Poppy stood in her socks in the living room and didn't bother to switch on any lamps. Instead, she followed the stairs, kicked off her jeans and her sweater and climbed numbly under the covers in Rafe's ginormous bed. Home and comfort and all the safe things she'd ever hoped for. The sounds of him moving around downstairs, bringing groceries in and following her upstairs comforted her because she didn't have the words even to say that she wanted him here by her side. But he knew, *he knew.*

She blinked slowly as he shrugged out of his jeans, that assessing study of his never wavering. He left his long johns on, climbed under the covers with her and wrapped his body around hers. And finally, she let the tension ease away.

He rubbed his hands over her back, slowly up and down. Goodness his hands were glorious. A person didn't need to talk when they were this amazing at communicating with action. How could he understand exactly what she needed, to be surrounded by his quiet steady presence?

"That was my house." She settled her cheek against his chest and spoke. "When I was a child. Here in Graciella." She let the constant sound of his heartbeat take her words. "I saw it when I first arrived. Someone was living there, I thought. But I haven't been back since. I... There's so much I don't know. So much happened when I was little. We left suddenly, and…and I never saw my dad again." *And all this time I thought he didn't want me.* How could she put those words out there aloud in the world?

"I never came back, Rafe." Admitting it was difficult. "Why did I never… And now it's empty. You saw it too, right? Something…feels wrong with me. I don't belong anywhere." The words seeped out from a deep wound.

"No." His deep voice calmed her. "No," he repeated. That hum of his heart matching the caress of his hand. "You're here now."

"Yeah," she agreed. "I don't know why though." Confused and exhausted, Poppy nestled in closer to Rafe's warmth, always his warmth. She closed her eyes and let him soothe her away into a dream.

Poppy's body settled as she sank deeper into sleep. Rafe was already recognizing her patterns. He was getting too close, feeling too much. It was all completely foreign to him, but how could he be any different around her? She shattered all his negative feelings, didn't seem to mind his anxiety with words, made him feel alive, connected, worthy. He wanted to comfort her. He wanted to bury himself in her body, sink into her soft welcoming beauty, but he couldn't. He *needed* to move, to work. Slipping out of bed, he made his way to the kitchen to get a few things ready for their dinner. Even that didn't settle his mind.

Eventually he tugged on his boots hoping his workshop might ease the pressure in his chest. *"I don't know why though."* Why were her words jagged knives cutting into him? *Because, idiot, you don't want her to be confused about why she's here.* He jogged the distance between the house and his shop. The swirling clouds and chilly wind make it feel more like nighttime than two in the afternoon. *Another storm's coming.* He could smell the snow in the air. Pretty, but not great for the animals or the damn plow he still hadn't managed to fix.

With each worry the sunlight slipped away from his grasp. *She* slipped away from his grasp. Only she was a person and was never his to keep in the first place.

Rafe readied his tools and the pieces of wood he'd picked out earlier. He turned the lights on over his desk and used the sketching to calm his mind, to organize his ideas. He'd be an idiot to use power tools right now, but the design would help him focus, help him rein in his unbridled emotions.

A long table for her sewing with a sleeve of drawers on one side, or a matching cabinet, where she could tuck away her sewing bits and pieces, so she wouldn't have to keep them in a ripped cardboard box spilling out around his place. Not that he minded her stuff. Jesus, he wanted her and her stuff all over.

She fit in that nook he'd built. She fit on his sofa, or trying to make breakfast in his kitchen with her soft pajamas on, her hair wild and gorgeous after a good night's sleep. She fit in his bed. She fit everywhere around his house, like he'd built it for her, for both of them. No, he didn't mind her stuff, which was its own kind of statement right there, for how he'd lived previously—completely organized, clutterless. Barren, if one wanted to call it that, perhaps. Rafe rubbed his chest. He was all turned inside out.

She deserved beauty and something solid. A home, a place to belong. Unique furniture for her own creations. A table, a pretty cabinet. He'd build it anyway, even if she wasn't planning on staying. She could take it with her when she went. A gift so she'd know she was worthy and loved and could belong anywhere.

Even if it wasn't here in simple Graciella with him.

* * * *

She found him in his shop. Her nap hadn't lasted long this time. She suspected the exhaustion had more to do with her emotions from this afternoon than any more lingering jet lag. He'd soothed her, tucked her in and let her rest. His note this time had been hastily written, *In the shop if you need me.*

There he is. He had his coat off and the sleeves of his black flannel rolled up. He was sitting at his high desk with his feet wrapped around the stool, his face as intent as the night she met him, when she'd screamed and tried to climb the wall. The image almost made her laugh now. Serious his expressions might be, but his heart was so open and giving, strong and soft at the same time. The kind she'd been searching for her entire life.

Did her heart fit with his? She wanted it to. It already reached out toward his to find the way they interlocked together. She wanted so dearly to trust their connection, to feel it click in place, but she was so afraid...that...that he didn't feel the same. He was so brilliant, smart and steady and settled. And she was a mess, really.

He was studying a paper under the lamplight and when he sensed her presence, turned his whole body her way, she felt and saw the soft smile, that barely there hint on his face, that thrilled her blood.

"Hi." She couldn't help her own smile, big and broad as he came to her, never wavering from that hot study of his, now aimed right at her. He set his hands on her hips and gently drew her to him.

"Hi." His gaze roamed over her face like an artist studying his canvas, or a doctor his patient, or a lover staking his claim. He was all of those in this moment, the creative soul, the caretaker, the fascinating lover. All hers, at least for now. And she was going to cling to every moment they had. "Better?" he asked, and she nodded.

"I never knew I was a napping person," she said with a bit of awe. But it was true. There was always something crucial to be done, even as a child—schoolwork, art classes, helping with dinner, chores. Naps were a luxury she'd never indulged in.

"Your body needed it."

Her body needed his. "I'm not sleepy anymore." She stood on her tiptoes and brushed her nose against his neck. God, she never knew wood could be sexy, but the scent on Rafe's clothes, on his neck, all over him did things to her. Lustful uninhibited things. Rafe's hands tightened on her hips.

"I promised you a-a-a…special dinner."

"Mm. It's only four-thirty. Not dinner time yet." Poppy untucked his shirt and roamed her hands over his muscles. "Darn long johns."

Rafe huffed out a laugh and took her hands away from his body.

Now it was her turn to laugh as he tugged her quickly across the walk and into the house. When they made it to his bedroom, he had his shirt unbuttoned and off before she could blink. She stepped into him. "I mean, I *love* these long johns." Her hands had a mind of their own, roaming over his chest, feeling his heat through the fabric. He had her so stirred up she was fumbling again.

"Yeah?" he asked and helped her with the buttons, then stood still as she pushed the long johns down, revealing all his powerful muscles. *Would it be weird to lick every single one?* She was having a hard time caring if it was weird or not.

"They are so hot," she whispered as he stepped out of them, nearly naked in only his boxer briefs. Her words caught in her throat. Was this really happening? Was this really her life right now? He shrugged out of his boxers, so nothing graced his body. This glorious, sexy man standing before her with eyes darkened to the night sky with desire for her. A dream. He didn't answer her unspoken questions with silly words. Who needed words in this moment? He whipped off her sweater and T-shirt in one whoosh. She hadn't bothered to put her bra back on. His eyes darkened as he trailed his fingers between her breasts to her jeans that he quickly helped her shimmy out of.

Rafe sucked in a breath. Oops, she'd already ditched her underwear too. If she hadn't, it would be soaked right now. Could one have an orgasm merely from the fiery stare of the sexiest person on the planet? The next thing she knew he'd grabbed her and lifted her so their bodies aligned. Poppy wrapped her legs around him and held on to his strong shoulders. Those shoulders were quickly becoming a favorite of hers.

His hands went right to her butt, digging into her skin so powerfully. *Such desperation.* His grip on her stripped away any lingering shyness or worries. All she wanted was to rub her body over his, so she did, trying to find the soothing to her aching skin, the burning need in her pussy, how her breath caught at the look in his eyes now.

She kissed him then, stole both their breaths, dove her tongue inside seeking all his warmth. He stumbled against the bed and sat with her on his lap. *Glorious. Oh yes.* She loved this, him naked spread out in front of her where she could inspect her way along his muscles and bones. She shimmied her body down so her knees straddled his sides and she had freedom to touch him everywhere. Roaming her hands over his skin, watching him watch her with that hooded, burning gaze. She kissed his chest, licked at his sweaty skin, tasted him. His scent lured her in. She sank to the floor in front of him. Rafe leaned up on his elbows nearly commanding her with the inferno in his eyes.

Poppy ran her fingers down his belly and over his shaft. She wrapped her hands around his length. *Powerful and hard.* Taking courage from the dark aching need in Rafe's eyes, she tasted him with her tongue and took him in her mouth, circling her tongue and sucking him deeper.

"Christ," he hissed and bucked against her.

It drew her on. It was everything she wanted, to make him lose control, give him as much pleasure as he'd wrung from her body. It felt like only seconds, as she sucked and pampered him, but her mind was lost in the fog. Who really knew how long it lasted before he swore again.

"Poppy. *Christ.*"

Suddenly she wasn't kneeling anymore as he lifted her and set her on his lap. He dragged her legs around him, fitting himself right at her core, and in one move, thrust into her wet, needy pussy. Rafe devoured her mouth, greedy for the connection, pouring all his need into her. And she took it, gave her own back to him, as their bodies crushed together. And when she tensed and pulsed around him, she rode out her orgasm on his lap, crying his name while he exploded into her, never letting go the tight hold he had around her. *Oh, my heart.*

Chapter Eighteen

"That was a…a really nice…uhm…"

"Shower?" Rafe helped her finish her sentence. He couldn't help his wide grin. Damn, he felt like smirking. And he wasn't a smirker. He might even pound his chest with the satisfaction bursting inside him. More than satisfaction… Fuck, was this what falling in love felt like?

"Everything." Poppy sighed, her smile meeting his. "Morning, day, nap, uhm…yeah and the shower too."

Wrapped in nothing but a towel, hair wet, face flushed and happy, she leaned against the bathroom counter as he pulled on his jeans. No long johns tonight. He didn't need the extra layer to have a cozy dinner with her. And he didn't need any extra barriers between them for…later. His own cheeks heated at the naked images. Who the hell was he? Having fantasies about a woman *while* he was with her, or *ever* for that matter. No woman had ever fascinated him so much.

Hell, he thought of her all the damn time. During the day, while buried inside her, in his dreams at night. His dreams were a whole other experience all together. Never had he imagined so vividly.

He could have her back in his bed right this minute if he wanted. His dick stirred at the damned fine thought. But he wanted to cook for her too, sit next to her at his corner table surrounded by windows, candles and music, and the fire going. He wanted to feel her thigh brush against his again and twine their fingers together whenever he craved her touch. Only the two of them, no interruptions, no responsibilities...no one else but them.

She ran a comb slowly through her hair, still watching him with that sated, lazy expression he'd put on her face. That they'd put on each other's faces. One stride was all it took to have her face cradled in his hands. He held her, carefully, but with intention, studying her face as the smile turned serious. Then he leaned in and kissed her, covered those lush lips with his, dove his tongue in to taste, to tangle, to speak all the words that were stuck in his throat. *Stay with me here. I'm falling in love with you. My heart is yours. I want a life with you.*

"I...I'm going to start dinner," he whispered and turned and walked away, hoping he hadn't ruined the moment.

What did he really know about relationships? How to be in one? How to hold on to one? How to even say that was what he wanted, what he hoped they were building. Maybe if he attacked it that way, as a thing to build, he could figure it out. Begin with a sketch of what he wanted, imagine, create, gather the materials and tools, carefully put them together until they became something beautiful and strong, and…and lasting.

Maybe I should calm down and start with dinner, build that and see if she likes it. Rafe calmed his breathing and began taking out the ingredients from the refrigerator. It was simple to make, really, but fun to eat. He'd first had beef fondue in college when a friend invited him to a party. Rafe had been overwhelmed. He couldn't get enough of the meat seared in hot oil and the selection of sauces to dip each piece in. He'd gone back to his tiny apartment that night and stayed awake for hours thinking of it, tasting it, mentally creating new dipping recipes. Over the years he'd perfected his own recipe.

This afternoon, when Poppy had fallen asleep, he'd made the sauces. Now all he had to do was cut the meat, heat the oil and make a salad. Working while she moved around upstairs made him dizzy with need. The table was set and when he lit the fire he could hear her singing, right before the sound of the hair dryer muffled her voice. He ran his hands along the smooth mantel, the piece of wood he'd sawed and sanded and set here above the hearth. He put his other hand to his chest, wondering if he could ease the foreign pain he felt there, wondering if he wanted to. Poppy made him feel things he'd never imagined, never even knew existed. Certainly never believed could be a part of his life.

"Wow," she whispered from the last step to the bottom.

Rafe's own *wow* leaped from his heart and got stuck in his throat. She wore a pretty peach dress with long floaty sleeves, but the rest barely came to her knees. Soft tights graced her legs, and she had a pair of his thick winter socks on over the tights. His eyes feasted.

"I...uhm...my feet were chilly. I hope you don't mind."

He shook his head. Took a step toward her, compelled by her. She thought she was cold, but she was wrong. She was all the light and warmth he needed. Before he could reach her, she floated toward the window on her cloud of beauty that knocked him sideways every time he set eyes on her.

"You did all this?" She brushed her hand through the air indicating the table. She gently fingered one of the candles. He'd turned the lights low, and now she glowed in candlelight. *Soft, sexy, mine.*

"I..." He stuck his hands in his pockets so he wouldn't grab her as she padded on her soft feet back to where he stood. He didn't want to always be grabbing her. He had to maintain control. But when she put her hands on his chest and leaned up to kiss him, the action was automatic. He wrapped his hands around her and held on. Her scent, floral and musky, shifted over him, blanketing him in one of his fantasies.

"Thank you," she whispered against his lips, the buzz of her words turning him on almost more than her kiss. His brain had left the building. "For dinner."

"Haven't eaten yet," he said, and she laughed, that deep, husky laugh of hers that fit her so damn well. Like the way she let loose when they made love. The way she devoured food. How she cooed over her fabrics. Even how she cherished her sewing machine. All of it with depth and flourish.

The only thing she held back with, he noticed, had to do with her place here in Graciella. What made her so skittish here? It was all tied up in her family, he suspected — her father, the old house they'd seen today, all the reasons she'd stayed away. The reason she'd returned. He could only see the pieces she allowed him to. Overall, she was an unfinished canvas and he wanted to uncover every secret part of her.

"I'm sure you made something delicious. You're amazing with your hands." She took his from around her and linked their fingers together, putting their chests flush.

He leaned to kiss her when he felt her stomach rumble against his, her laughter following again. And even though he hadn't made it to her lips yet, he couldn't help but smile when she said, "I think I am hungry again."

"Mm." Rafe walked her to the kitchen. "Good. Here." He moved her to the cutting board, put the knife in her hand, brushed the hair away from her neck and left one long lingering kiss against her soft skin, capturing her scent.

"I get to help?" Her voice was full of awe, breathless, and damn, he couldn't wait till later. He stepped away before he ruined her dress and their dinner, his mind a hive of lust and desire.

"You trust me? With your tools?" Poppy held the knife but gave him an eyebrow wiggle.

His smile grew. He almost hurt from how much he'd smiled in the last few days. "I trust you." The words were more serious than he intended.

Rafe stepped away from her and made their plates with the meat and sauces while Poppy cut the tomatoes and cucumber for the salads. He sliced the baguette, warm from the oven, putting it on the table with the softened butter. He heated the oil in the fondue pot and opened a bottle of red wine while trying to shove away that rapid-fire worry lancing his thoughts at the fact he'd told her he trusted her. And wondering if she understood how much he meant with one simple phrase.

"This night is lovely," Poppy said, sitting down to eat. She squeezed Rafe's hand. "You did all this, candles, fancy dinner, fire. Oh! It's even snowing again."

Rafe, sexy and cute at the same time with the embarrassed blush taking over his sculpted cheekbones, shook his head and gave her a loopy grin. Damn the man looked good grinning at her.

"I didn't m-m-make it snow, Poppy."

The soft way he said her name. She swooned again. It must have been a sex haze, fabulous nap, amazing shower, kiss-swollen lips, Rafe's voice-induced swoon.

"I love how it sparkles in the Christmas lights. How peaceful. I haven't seen snow this heavy in years. Graciella welcomed me with all this beauty, and it feels so safe, my own personal cocoon. I never want it to end." *I don't ever want to leave here.*

"Mm." Rafe studied her. His gaze was hotter than the flames in the fire and she basked in it. "Want me to show you how?" he asked, holding out a fondue fork with a piece of meat on it.

"Yes, please." She was swoony, but she was also starving. Again. And Rafe had cooked for her. Again. "This is amazing," she said as the meat sizzled in the oil, cooking in mere seconds.

"Now, careful," Rafe said and demonstrated how to dip the meat in a sauce and carefully bite it without burning one's lips on the hot fondue fork.

Oh my God, his mouth is so sexy. Now it was her turn. She carefully mimicked him. *Then,* talk about swoon— "Amazing!" she exclaimed.

Poppy closed her eyes and savored the flavors of the charred meat and the tarragon-flavored creamy sauce she'd chosen first. He fit another piece of meat on his fork and dipped it in the oil. She copied him again a few times, loving how the candles' glow highlighted his strong fingers, how he spread the butter on his bread, the way he sipped his wine and smiled at her.

She followed, tasting the delicious red wine he'd poured her, slathering her bread with butter. Her tastebuds puckered over the simple but delicious salad with his shallot dressing. Every flavor burst on her tongue.

Eventually the oil, heated by a flame of canned heat underneath, cooled enough that it took longer for each piece of meat to cook, as their bellies filled. Along with their hearts—at least her heart. She couldn't know for certain what he was feeling, but his eyes and his expressions sure told a very specific tale, that he liked being here with her, that he wanted her. The quiet of the cooling oil became such a lovely background for them to talk, and laugh and sigh at each other, Rafe offering as much as she did to the conversation which indicated to her that he was feeling comfortable. Maybe sex did his body good too. She giggled at the thought.

"What's funny?" He nudged her arm with his elbow. They sat in his lovely window corner nook, right next to each other.

And all through dinner she'd been able to feel his heat.

"I'm full of so many emotions, I think, or sex bloom, or both," she teased, although her heart nudged her that it wasn't teasing. His eyes heated at her words. "I love this dinner, Rafe. It's one you make for people you care about."

"Hm." He put his last piece of meat in to cook. "I haven't...ever... I haven't made it for anyone."

When he looked away and sighed, Poppy hoped she hadn't ruined the evening. All his calm and relaxed vibes slipped away, replaced by a tension she couldn't understand.

Overcome suddenly with so many feelings, Poppy swallowed and tried not to let any tears fall. "No one?" she whispered. "Why?" Oh shoot, she hadn't meant to blurt that last part out, like he was a weirdo. He wasn't. Or if he was, he was hers. Her weird, hot, brilliant person. At least she wanted him to be. More than anything. More than ever.

"Haven't, uhm...wanted to." He rubbed his hands on his jeans before he faced her again. "For anyone. Before...you. There's all this time..." He gestured between them. "For talking in between the cooking."

The fear that washed over his face when he said *talking* softened her into a pile of mush. She was mushy in love with this man. *I've never ever been in love before.* Poppy kissed him then. She couldn't help it. She didn't want to lose what she was feeling in this moment. It was all so precious. This beautiful shy man made the most romantic dinner for her, despite his fear of talking. Or maybe because of it.

He kissed her back, gripping her waist as she turned into him. She suddenly couldn't get close enough to him. *Too many clothes.* Poppy tried to climb on his lap, but he stopped her.

"Wait." He set her gently aside, put the flame out under the fondue pot. Then he carefully carried it into the kitchen. "I don't want you to get burned."

Sliding back onto the bench, he hauled her over so she was straddling him. Kneeling over him, her hair floating around them, the fire burning between them, she'd never felt so beautiful, so cherished.

He slid his hands up her thighs, bringing her dress up so he could grip her ass. He ran his strong hands over her silky tights and she nearly came with the pleasure of him caressing her while she rubbed her pelvis against him. He helped her move even closer, pulling her body into his, while she raked her hands through his hair and brought her mouth to his. She let all her inhibitions float away and arched into him over and over, devouring his mouth, licking at him. He swept his warm hands down her back and suddenly he stood, lifting her and carrying her to the couch. He set her down and pulled away.

"Don't go," she pleaded.

Chapter Nineteen

"You're always asking me not to go… I…I never want to leave you." His words were harsh with desire. Even he could hear the desperation. He turned the lights off and brought the small candles to the coffee table. Then he tossed a few more logs on the fire. "Candlelight, and fire, and…" He pointed toward the window. "Snow."

"Won't anyone be able to see us?"

Shy now, was she?

He shook his head, almost not caring if anyone happened to walk by. He felt full of power, feral for her. Need simmered through his body. But he also would never embarrass her. "No one will be out in this." Desire gave him confidence, spurred him on. He climbed over her on the couch and stretched out his body onto hers.

He wanted her naked, wanted them both naked, but he also wanted to kiss her all night, like this, her body under his, her arms around him, snuggled in their own secret hideaway. "So beautiful," he said and traced her bottom lip with his thumb. Even with his weight on her, she lifted her pelvis into him, seeking that same friction he craved.

She pulled out his shirt from his waistband and started to undo his buttons. "No long johns," she whispered.

And the awe in her gaze when she studied him made him want to bow to her. She hid nothing with her expressions and he'd never in his life had someone gaze at him with such worship.

"I love those long johns," she whispered. "But wow, am I glad there's nothing between this shirt and your body right now." She ran her nose and lips along his chest. "You smell so good, Rafe."

Rafe kissed her neck and ran his hands down her body to that heavenly spot under her dress. In one swift motion, he had her dress over her head, tossing it over the back of the sofa and devoured her laughter, kissing her like she was everything brilliant in the world. Because she was.

"Oh, your hands are so warm." She shimmied out of her bra while he stroked her arms, her fingers, her neck, lost in her skin. She took his hands and placed them on her naked breasts, arching into his grip, and moaning. He needed to be inside her while she made those sounds.

Rafe rid himself of his jeans and boxers and as carefully as he could without ripping them, slid her shimmery tights off her legs, drooling at the fact she had no underwear on. His sexy sneak, creating new ways to drive him wild. This time when he came back to her, he smoothed his hands all over her curves, along her soft belly. He palmed her breasts again and, watching her eyes, tongued one nipple in his mouth to lavish his attention on, kissing and sucking while she writhed and moaned under him. *She definitely blushes all over. So fucking gorgeous.*

"Rafe," she squealed when he gently raked her nipple with his teeth. "Do that again."

He did, soothing each bite with his tongue then moving on to the other breast. She squirmed and rubbed against him, begging for more. Exactly how he felt. He was so hard against her soft body. Sparks shot down his spine. He wasn't going to last long.

"Ready?" he asked as he lined their bodies up.

"So ready." Her eyes were closed, her face washed in bliss.

She was slick and warm, waiting for him to enter her, inviting him with her movement and now her words.

And slowly, while dragging his lips up her chest to her neck, he slid in, inch by agonizing, beautiful inch. And when he was fully seated in her and could feel her pussy holding him there, he pulled one of her legs around him. Then he tangled his hand between them so he could play with her clit and give her more pleasure.

He set his lips on hers. "Open your eyes," he whispered.

And she did. The flames in her gaze met his immediately. She wrapped her hands around him, connecting them even more. Then he kissed her while he moved inside her, never letting her gaze go, trying to will all the words and emotions he was feeling into her body. Love and desire, heart and body, now and forever.

"I feel…" She stilled and clamped around him.

He rubbed her clit and sped up his thrusts. He was being taken over by her body.

"Amazing, Rafe." She cried out his name and came apart around him.

And Rafe buried his head in her neck and lost himself in her again.

Rafe's emotions lodged in his throat, even as he tried to catch his breath. He shifted slightly to the side but kept them connected. *"Don't go,"* she'd pleaded. Never. He never wanted to be separated from her, from her light, her love. He craved her essence. What would it be like to be loved by her?

"Wow." She snuggled into him and whispered, "What you do to me... Wow."

He felt the same. His body floated on the high.

"You make me feel so special, Rafe." Poppy ran her hand gently along his back, her eyes drifting closed.

Rafe pulled the throw blanket over them and memorized that soft unguarded smile on her face as she fell asleep. When the fire eventually died, he carried her to bed and tucked them in together, listening to the whimpering sounds she made as she dreamed. Rafe stayed awake for hours imagining a future, a life with Poppy. For some reason, he was worried if he fell asleep along with her, this would never be true. So instead, he concentrated his imagination into a vision of the two of them together, here in Graciella forever.

* * * *

Mm. I much prefer waking up with Rafe than alone. Poppy stretched out on the bed, feeling around to find no sexy Rafe with her. Disappointment sank in her belly. Such a big, lonely bed when she was the only one in it. And she'd never thought of a bed as lonely before. She smiled and let last night float around her mind. Happy, yet bummed at the same time. Bummed because he was gone. Happy because last night had been incredible. She'd felt wrapped in a romantic golden bubble. Full of so much desire. Desire Rafe had satisfied deliciously on the couch.

Who even am I? She giggled into her pillow again. Sex had never been not only so amazing during, but making her desire it, again and again with Rafe. She couldn't keep her hands to herself. And it felt the same for him like he had to be touching her, kissing her, petting her. *Ahh.* As if he had eyes and hands and desire only for her. And that knowledge was powerful.

He is the one person I want to be with most in the world. How had that all happened so quickly? She didn't understand, and she almost didn't want to investigate the why. She wanted to bask in the fact that it felt true. Her heart had fluttered open around him, more and more with each moment, until eventually it had stepped forward and claimed him.

At some point in the night, Rafe must have carried her to bed. Darn it, and she'd totally missed it. There was something primal in a naked, strong Rafe carrying her to bed, all his powerful muscles on display. He wouldn't have bothered to put on clothes, would he? No. Although that wasn't a hardship to imagine either. His shirt hanging open, jeans unbuttoned while he held her close to him and carried her gently upstairs. Why, why, why did she have to sleep so soundly? And that was odd in itself, because she'd never slept that well before. Another tidbit to tuck into her soul.

It was going to be a beautiful day. She grinned when she saw the huge mug on the bedside table. Her thoughtful man. Beside the mug was another lovely note from Rafe. *I wonder what he'd say if I told him his notes are cute?* Another giggle made its way out of her. *Oh, I can't wait to tease him with that later. Maybe I'll get a grumpy frown out of him.* Then she'd have to kiss the frown right off. Poppy fanned her face. She was getting heated up imagining all the ways she could kiss him. How hungrily he'd dive into that kiss.

Had to go help at the barns. I'll find you later...Rafe

Poppy brought the note to her mouth and gave it a soft kiss. It even smelled like Rafe. She set her mug and the note on the table and slid under the covers. She wished he were here right now. Poppy ran her hands over her body, naked, warm, turned on. *I want Rafe's hands to be caressing me.* She closed her eyes. *Such beautiful, strong hands.* All the better to worship her with.

She felt naughty as she let her fingers stray to her pussy. But Rafe seemed to like it when she was naughty. And that thought brought a flush over her aching needy body. Even her nipples were hard and ready for his touch. She rubbed her wetness and found her clit. Poppy closed her eyes and imagined Rafe standing there in his long johns watching her pleasure herself. All that smoldering burning possession on his face. He could unbutton those long johns and stroke his cock that would be so, *so* hard for her. And maybe, maybe she'd touch the tip and make him groan. She whimpered with the image, with need. Her body arched as her orgasm crashed over her with images of Rafe, devouring her.

* * * *

It was such a gorgeous day. Poppy practically skipped to the main house. She hadn't seen anyone else besides Rafe in two days. She kind of wished they could stay in their bubble for weeks and weeks, until spring came and the sun lasted longer in the sky. Even with it warming the land today, it still rested mostly low on the horizon, casting its fingerprints for only a few hours. Poppy didn't mind so much because she felt bright and warm within. Nothing in the world could bring her down now.

Also, she couldn't get over how gorgeous and magical the land looked covered in new snow under a soft blue sky. She'd never tire of it. The scene, the bracing crisp air, the peacefulness of a sunny day in winter — it all created this aura around her. One big, graceful meditation allowing her mind to settle and breathe. The land twinkled around her, like the wedding the other night with all the sparkling lights and dresses and decorations. She really had been surrounded by lovely shimmering things since she'd arrived in Graciella.

Paris had felt like this once, or had it? She'd dreamed of living in Paris ever since she'd gotten to visit the city when she graduated from high school. But visiting and trying to make a living in a city were two different experiences. And for the last two years she'd been barely scraping by financially, emotionally, groundedly. Was that a thing? She'd never found her foundation, her steadiness living and working there.

It might have been the job, hah! The slave labor in the most competitive design house ever. It might have been her horrible nasty boss. It might have been that the closest friendship she'd made was with a hundred-year-old neighbor with an ancient cat who hardly ever even spoke to Poppy. It might have been that even though she worked in the fashion world, she hadn't felt one bit creative.

Paris was a beautiful sparkly city, sometimes. She just wasn't certain it was ever really meant to be hers. And honestly, as she slowed her pace, she couldn't even remember if Paris had ever really been her dream, or her mom's dream for her. She'd had inklings of that thought for years, but had shoved it aside for the same reason she'd said to her mom on the phone the other night, that she was afraid of doing something to make her mom not want her. Because all these years she'd told herself her dad hadn't wanted her at all. That was the narrative she'd been living with. Poppy sucked in a breath. *I've been assuming no one would ever want me, living my life closed off and focused only on my career.*

Fleeing here from Paris, alone, scared and exhausted, had shattered the façade she'd been living behind in so many ways. And even with the new knowledge of her dad's death and the heartbreak it opened in her, she still felt renewed in a way. Open to figuring out what *she* really wanted in life, not what her mother or anyone else wanted for her. She wanted to create beautiful clothes and sell them, share that love of fashion with the world.

Being back here, being around her cousins, them treating her as if she'd never left, seeing her old house, the beautiful snow, weddings and the Christmas holiday season, simple things like napping, sewing again for joy, being cooked and cared for, Rafe. Amazing sex and…more than that. *Love.* It embraced her. And even more amazing, it poured out of her for a special human being she'd never even dreamed could be hers. Rafe reached in and nudged her deep hidden longings with his magic, his trust, his beauty. She'd never felt so amazing in her life, hadn't imagined it was possible.

Poppy paused at the crest of the hill. The main Brockman House stood in all her grand glory, surrounded by low rolling waves of snow-covered ground. The snow-white branches of the apple orchard glistened. Rafe's house was behind her and Adam and Cassandra's not too far beyond that. From here she could see past the land to the ocean. A sparkling white landscape. This entire farm was on a new path, a new beginning. *A new beginning for me too.* She laughed and twirled, giddy with joy, with hope. Beautiful things simmered all around her and within her and she was determined to grab hold of all of them.

Reaching the main house and entering through the kitchen door felt cozy and wonderful. Another way she maybe belonged here. Not a stranger or a guest, but family. Beloved family who could drop by whenever she wanted, or when her aunt had called and invited her over for lunch. The fun but busy chaos of the wedding and all its festivities and guests had ended. And as lovely as it had been to be swept up in all of that, Poppy was grateful for the calm now, and for maybe getting to spend more quality time with her cousins and their families, and her aunt, here in Graciella. A place she was suspecting she didn't want to leave.

"Aunt Katie?" Poppy kicked her boots off and left them on the back porch. "I'm here," she called and pushed through the door. The kitchen's steamy goodness enveloped her with its savory and delicious scents. There was a hint of garlic and tomato. Her stomach, never one to be bashful around food, rumbled. Katie was at the large island adding cream to a large pot. She smiled her soft, knowing smile when she noticed Poppy. But then she turned toward the table.

"*Mom?*" Poppy stopped where she was and glanced between her aunt and her mother. A niggle of worry shivered through her spine. "What...what's going on?"

Chapter Twenty

"Hi, honey." Her mom, glamorous as ever in stylish gray wool pants and a soft cream cashmere sweater, her hair up the way she usually wore it, in a chignon, stood from her seat at the table. Pearls graced her ears, her makeup expertly applied.

Poppy had barely added a hint of lip gloss to her own lips this morning. Lips that had still been beautifully swollen from Rafe's late-night kisses. She'd brushed her fingers over her mouth, capturing the memory of his touch.

Pausing at first, then recovering her graceful self, her mother walked toward Poppy and wrapped her in a hug. It took Poppy a few seconds to engage. Expensive perfume, subtle but familiar in her mother's clothes, reached her and Poppy softened into the embrace, holding on, closing her eyes and letting the familiarity comfort her. It had been so long since she'd had a hug from her mom.

"What are you doing here?" Poppy pulled away, remembering that she was still hurt and confused by the fact that her mom had withheld vital information. Poppy had asked for space, but had she really simply been hiding? Maybe it was time now to get it all out in the open. Face to face on the same continent.

"I wanted to come sooner, but—"

"I know how busy you are, Mom." This had been a truth between them for as long as Poppy could remember. Keeping busy, always doing more to get further ahead in their careers, in their lives. Poppy had followed in her mom's footsteps in that area. But *busy* sure could hide a lot of things, like being vulnerable and authentic emotions.

"No." Her mom shook her head, then gave a soft laugh. "I would have been here after that first phone call, but I couldn't get a flight right away. And when I told Will. He..." Her mom's smile grew at the mention of Poppy's stepdad. "He asked me to wait for him, so he could come too."

"Will's here?" Her mom's face softened again, and Poppy was struck by how beautiful her mom was. Poppy had known it all her life, but it had seemed like an unattainable part of her mother. Now, the loveliness shone through, especially when she talked about Will.

A memory stole through Poppy's mind. Her mom, so much younger, crying, yelling at her dad, and her dad unhappy or angry. It was hard to tell from a fuzzy memory. He'd stood on the porch of their old home. Poppy had been nine or ten. She'd been sitting at their kitchen table and her mom had shut the door in her dad's face. Poppy didn't get another glimpse of her mother that night as Anne had turned and walked away, shutting herself in her bedroom.

A shiver ran through Poppy, like a ghost.

"He's having a peek in town. You know how he is with old buildings and reconstruction."

"Yes." Poppy tried to smile, but there was a weird feeling in the room, hovering over them.

"Why don't you two have a seat and I'll bring you soup," Katie said.

Anne ushered Poppy into the built-in, rubbing her hand.

"I was so surprised when Annie called and said she was here, in Graciella." Katie set bowls in front of them.

Annie? Another memory. Aunt Katie had always called her mom Annie when they'd lived here. Katie was the only one who ever dared. Poppy's mom was Anne Emilia Bergstrom to everyone else. Polished, put together, old money, successful interior designer...wife of billionaire Will Bergstrom.

"I'm sorry I didn't call you back," Poppy started. "I...I..." She sucked in a breath. "I didn't think you—"

Her mom gripped Poppy's hand. "That I cared enough to come be with you after what happened to you in Paris and after that last phone call we had?"

Poppy shook her head and willed the tears to stay put. "No, not cared...I didn't think you'd come."

"You're my daughter, Poppy. And you're upset with me, I understand that, but I was so worried. And we didn't leave things okay on the phone. There's so much more to tell you."

"I was going to call..." Would she have called her mom back? Would she have been brave enough? She believed so, but it also felt nice having Anne drop all her responsibilities and come to Poppy.

"I heard about the wedding." Anne glanced at Katie. "It sounds like it was wonderful."

"It really was," Poppy said. "But I...I also needed time and space, Mom." She had needed time to think, not that she'd done a lot of that in the last two days unless it involved dreaming of Rafe and an inkling of a life here in Graciella.

"I understand, honey." Her mom gently pushed a lock of Poppy's hair away from her cheek. Her mom's face was so serious. And Poppy felt that odd stirring again, a foreboding. "You've always been one to take a long time to process things. And you've always done it silently, in your own head." Anne dropped her hand from Poppy's cheek and Poppy missed the contact immediately. Her mom sipped her water. Anne's hand was shaking. *Is she nervous? Did I do that? Did I make her nervous?*

"I also didn't want to have the rest of our conversation on the phone." Now her mom faced Poppy directly. "You're mad I didn't tell you about your father. And I didn't. Right away."

Right away? Poppy looked between her mom and her aunt again, as if there was a link between the two women with information that would clue Poppy in to what was going on.

"The other night on the phone, what I told you was the truth. I didn't tell you about your dad right away because I was so worried you would think it was your fault. But after you started therapy and were doing well, months later your grandmother and I decided it was time to tell you the truth. So we did."

"What?" All the blood drained from Poppy's face.

"Yes." Anne nodded. "You didn't have much of a reaction. It was...well, it scared us. You listened and said you understood, then you walked away. When we tried to bring it up, you got angry and shoved us away.

Your therapist said the same. And" — her mother let out a deep breath — "this is where I truly failed you. We eventually quit asking. All of us.

"You were such an old soul for your age, we always said. And at the time I guess I thought it was your way of dealing with it. It was selfish of me. You started doing so well in school and with your art. I thought we were getting close again. I never acknowledged this massive trauma we both shoved in a box and closed behind us. I had *no* idea until our conversation the other night that you'd shut it so far away you didn't remember at all. Or that you thought for one second your dad didn't love you to pieces."

All the air in her chest was suddenly gone, sucked away, swirling her into the past. Poppy nearly doubled over at the impact. "What? How...how can I not remember?" Her voice was shaky.

Her aunt sat beside her and set a mug of tea down. "Here, Poppy. Maybe this will help."

Poppy wrapped her hands around the mug, soaking in the heat, but it only went so far. The rest of her body was ice. It was the type of sharp cold that hurt all the way to her bones. Worse than Paris where she'd been both without heat and afraid. This was different altogether.

"I've been talking to a psychologist, and she said sometimes our brains do that, put a trauma away. Make us forget it ever happened in the first place. It's a form of survival mechanism at the time."

"But something so important. I feel...I feel..." Her stomach rolled. Her face was hot and sweat beaded around her forehead. All her memories churned to get out. The times her mom had asked if she wanted to talk about her dad and how poorly Poppy had reacted. How she used to wake in the middle of the night, scared of the dark, so she'd turn all her lights on and draw and paint. Art had always soothed her. Poppy grabbed her water glass and held it to her head.

"I never knew you believed your dad didn't want you, Poppy. I'm so, so sorry. That's the farthest thing from the truth."

"Really?" Poppy asked. Her mom nodded. They were both crying now. "He loved you so much. So, *so* much. He, um, well there's more I haven't told you yet. He left you the house in Graciella, our old house. I found a management company to rent it until you were ready for it. I should have told you sooner. As the years went by, I didn't know how."

Her mom set an envelope on the table in front of Poppy. Poppy put her hand on it and drew it close. It was plain, a boring legal envelope for mailing with the clasp folded closed. With shaking fingers, she gently opened it and withdrew a small stack of papers. They were legal papers with small print. Words floated before Poppy's blurry vision. Paperclipped to the bottom was a smaller blue envelope with her name on it in her father's writing.

"He must have written it right away." Her mom's voice caught on the last word. Clearing her throat, Anne continued, "It arrived in the mail the day after he died. I didn't know what to do with it…well when we both went into denial. I put it with the papers from the lawyer when they arrived after his estate was settled."

Poppy's mom was speaking but the words sounded as though coming through a deep dark tunnel. Poppy opened the envelope and a note fell out.

"'Love muffin.'" Poppy traced the handwriting. *Love muffin* had been what her dad called her when he sang to her.

I'm so sorry. I should have taken much better care of our family, of your mom, of our love, of you. I want you to know how much I love you and how much I always will. You will always be the best and brightest thing that ever flew into my life. Better than any art or music I could create. I hope you can forgive me. And I can't wait to see you and hug you soon. Love, Daddy O, forever.

She'd called him Daddy O. And that memory rushed her like too much noise on a screaming flying roller coaster. She covered her ears and shook her head. "No, no…I…" The words drowned in her gut. "He loved me?" It was a stolen whisper, a question. The pieces didn't fit together. Or maybe it was her heart shattering all over again. The pain was unbearable. A spinning sensation swirled around her.

"Poppy," her mother called from far away. Too far.

"Adam." Katie's voice sounded weird. She was on her phone. "Is Rafe with you?"

Rafe?

"Send him to the main house now. It's Poppy. She needs him. Be quick."

Chapter Twenty-One

"So, you and Poppy, huh?" Adam elbowed Rafe as they made their way on foot through the snow. The path was clear, but the snow was more fun, shoving and running and tossing snowballs at each other. *More fun.* Those were the kinds of thoughts Rafe had been having since Poppy came into his life. *Fun, playful, intense, confusing.* Things certainly weren't boring anymore, or rigid. And Rafe loved it, loved finding hints of Poppy around his house. Some things were out in the open, others, he enjoyed searching for.

This morning two spools of thread rested on top of the coffee maker. She must have left them when she was searching for a snack. He'd set them back near her machine. He'd wanted to sneak one into his pocket to feel her closer to him when he was at work. The note she'd left him had been tucked against the windowsill above the sink.

"Yeah," he said. That was all he said. Not that he didn't trust Adam and want to talk over his feelings. He did, actually. But how to voice the massiveness of it all? Cass and Willow and their babies were at a playdate in town today, so when Adam and Rafe had finally finished fixing the snowplow, they'd decided to grab Poppy and head to the main house for lunch. Adam had seen her note first.

Rafe. I hope your morning was lovely. I missed you. But thank you for making me coffee. I'm headed to see Aunt Katie at the main house. Yours, Poppy.

Two little heart drawings followed.

Rafe had barely been able to take it all in before Adam's grin grew wide and he started in on him. First it was teasing. But now that they'd settled into a walk, Adam's question felt serious. If Rafe needed examples of men in his life who were seriously in love with their women, the Brockman brothers were the epitome. When Rafe had first arrived in Graciella, he had seen what they all had, but never believed *he* could have something so amazing.

Now more than ever, he wanted a soulmate, a family, love. He wanted to belong to Poppy O'Brien. He didn't need to ask Adam how he'd known Cass was the one, because Rafe already sensed Poppy was his belonging. What he wanted help understanding was whether or not he was doing things right. He wanted to create a space she might love to be in with him. But whenever he started, the words, as usual, backed up like a traffic jam in his head.

Rafe stopped in the snow. "I'm lost."

Adam turned from where he'd walked ahead. "Uh, pretty sure you're not."

Rafe shook his head. He and Poppy weren't a secret. Adam had seen the note. Anyone could have seen him dancing with Poppy at the wedding, leaving hand in hand with her. Yet, it still felt sacred sharing what was between them with anyone else. He had no idea how they'd take it. "I mean, with...with...with Poppy." He wanted to avoid Adam's gaze, but he was the first good friend Rafe had had in a long time. He trusted Adam.

Adam didn't smile then. Instead, he stepped closer and focused. "I knew what you meant. I don't think you're lost at all. I think you've found a person you care for and you're showing her that. I've seen the way you treat people, even before Poppy came. You're a good man and you deserve to find someone special. We've all seen you and Poppy together." Adam grinned. "I don't think I've ever seen you smile so much. And Poppy, well, she looks at you the way Cass and Willow and the boys look at me."

"Yeah?" Rafe's throat was tight. His chest swelled with emotion.

"Like I'm the sunshine that brightens their days."

"Poppy's the sun. She's...she...she warms my days."

"Yeah," Adam said and gripped his shoulder. "That's the truth of it, isn't it. Really, it's their love that makes our hearts beat."

That was exactly how Rafe felt. His emotions had kicked into gear the minute he'd set eyes on Poppy. His brain might have been confused as to why the hell a stranger was in his bed, but his heart had leaped right up and said, "*Mine*."

"Thank you," Rafe said.

"Anytime, man."

"You...uhm, you're good with them."

"Cass and the kids?" Adam's smile stretched wide.

Rafe nodded.

"Thank you. That's the best compliment ever. I didn't have a good example."

They started walking again as the wind kicked and blew around them. Rafe knew bits and pieces about the late TD Brockman and what a horrible man he'd been. Worse than Rafe's own father, whose biggest crime was being absent. Maybe, if Adam and his brothers could find such genuinely happy and healthy relationships, then Rafe could too.

It shifted his mindset out of the doom-and-gloom belief that he was meant to be alone in life. He'd always been, even when his mom had been alive. She'd had one foot in Mexico waiting for his dad to come back, living a life of useless hope and *if onlies*. Rafe wanted to live in the here and now. He wanted to be worthy of Poppy. He wanted her to want to be with him. It was a fragile thing, hope.

They'd crested the hill from the orchard to the main house when Adam's phone rang.

"Hey, Mom. Yeah. Got it." Adam hung up and said, "Something's wrong with Poppy, they need you."

Adam started running, but it took a few seconds for Rafe's brain to catch up with the stumble his heart experienced. When it did, he ran through the snow like his life depended on it, because it did. In less than two weeks, she'd become his oxygen. Fear urged him on faster than he'd ever run before, sucking in deep breaths of frozen air, following the call beating inside his chest.

His nerves were a mess of worry when he rushed into the kitchen, imagining every horrible scenario. *Is she hurt? How badly?* Had they called an ambulance? His fear and worry swirled together into a tornado when he saw her sitting there so small and fragile. "Poppy?" he hushed out through his massive breaths.

And when she turned the anguish on her face nearly brought him to his knees.

"Rafe?"

He slid into the booth beside her, afraid, as if she might break to pieces before his eyes. But Poppy took all the guesswork away when she flopped her head onto his shoulder, as if she could barely hold it up anymore, as if she needed him.

"You came. I... Can you...? I need..."

A woman was next to Poppy, holding Poppy's hand and saying her name. And Katie was there, trying to soothe the woman.

"Take her home, Rafe," Katie said to him. "She needs you."

Rafe didn't hesitate. He scooped Poppy into his arms. Hers sagged between them onto her lap. In his grip, she flopped like a ragdoll, strung out, no energy. *What the fuck had happened?*

"I don't feel good," she said in a small voice. "I'm freezing."

"Here," Katie said and tucked Poppy's coat around her.

He didn't speculate on why they'd called him or how they knew he'd come, or how they knew she'd want him. He didn't worry what anyone thought. His only concern was her. And as carefully as he could, Rafe raced to his house with Poppy tucked in his arms.

"Here," he said when he made it inside and set her on the sofa.

"I'm so... I'm shaking, Rafe."

"Gonna get the fire go-go-going." He dragged the blanket over. Once he was certain the logs had caught, he kicked off his boots, climbed behind Poppy on the couch and tucked her into his side. He tangled her legs under his and wrapped his arms around her. Poppy turned in his arms to face him and buried her head in his chest.

"What hap-happened?" he asked, gently finding her soft fingers and rubbing heat into them.

"My dad's dead. He died a long time ago." She spoke through the sobs that racked her body.

"Poppy." His voice was rough. Why was it always so fucking difficult to find the words, to make them work? He held her and let her cry, wiped her tears with his hands, placed a gentle kiss on her head. A shiver made its way through her, and she snuggled even closer to him. Her sobs had quieted but her words were so soft, strained.

"All this time I knew. That's the worst part, but my brain hid it from me. I don't understand. And he...he left me a note, Rafe."

"That's good, right?" Rafe gave her a small smile, knowing how much she appreciated notes.

"It's... It was... He sent it a long time ago. There's so much I need to tell you."

"It's okay. We have time. All the time in the world."

"I used to believe that, but what if we don't?" She gripped his shirt with the same passion she'd infused into her words.

That rocked Rafe to the core. What did she mean? Was she leaving soon? Did she not want to stay here the way he wanted her to?

"I thought he didn't love me. I always thought." She was drifting in and out with her words, and Rafe wasn't sure he was following her correctly. "But he did, Rafe." Poppy rested her hands against his chest.

"He did what?"

"He loved me."

Fuck, that broke him. How could she ever have doubted that? Had she spent a lifetime with that thought poisoning her mind? That her father hadn't loved her? If he hadn't the man had been worse than a fool. *You've believed the same thing all these years.* It was different for him. Rafe's father had never been in his life. Poppy's had and when he wasn't anymore it was because he'd died. Not because he was too lazy and irresponsible to come see his kid.

"Of course he did."

She gave a small huff and wiped tears from her cheek. "We've both lost someone." Poppy placed a kiss against his chest, comforting him even when she was the one in need.

"Yeah," he agreed, too spun out of orbit to say anything else about losing his mom. Mostly he felt like he'd never had his mom. They did have that in common — the absence of a parent for so long.

"You're...you're always so warm." Shivers still ran through her body.

He hated that she was shivering. "I've got you."

"Okay. I trust you." Poppy snuggled in deeper.

Chapter Twenty-Two

Poppy studied her surroundings for a few minutes. She lay on the couch in Rafe's living room. The fire glowed in front of her. Low light streamed through the windows. None of which was far from the realm of possibility. It was the rest of the scene that pricked at her brain and made her question whether or not she was in some weird foreign universe, where one's worlds collided. It wasn't the first time she'd woken in his house disconcerted. And it wasn't the first time she'd been alone when it had happened. It was, however, the first time she'd woken in his house, with her feet tucked against her mom.

Anne sat at the other end of Rafe's massive couch with her feet on the ottoman, a soft throw over her legs, glasses on, and she was…knitting? There was no phone glued to her mom's ear, no business table strewn with designs and work-related documents. *Hm?* The flicker of a candle caught Poppy's eye. It sat on the coffee table, giving off a subtle rich scent of bergamot, her mom's favorite.

Can I smell in my dreams?

"You're awake," her mom said.

"I am?" Poppy asked, and Anne gave a soft laugh. Poppy couldn't remember the last time she'd heard that sound coming from her mom. Or maybe Poppy hadn't ever paid enough attention to notice. She chewed on that thought for a moment. Apparently, she was aces at living in a narrowminded coil of truths in her life. "Knitting? Who are you and what have you done with my mother?" Poppy nudged her toes against her mother's hip. She tried for lightheartedness.

The foundation had shifted between the two of them and Poppy was uncertain how to proceed. She only knew her brain, body and heart felt wrung out, exhausted. And perhaps part of that was from trying to live a life inauthentically. Ignoring hard things hadn't done her any good.

Anne set her knitting on her lap and settled her gaze on Poppy. Gone was her serene expression. Worry lined her forehead. "I've been knitting for years, Poppy. It helps me relax. And I love all the new wool and wool blends and colors people are creating. It's nice to have a creative outlet for myself."

"I'm sorry," Poppy said as her tears welled up again.

Her mom gripped her foot. "You have nothing to be sorry for, darling. We failed you. I...I had no idea all these years that you thought he didn't want you, didn't love you. I'm so, so sorry."

It was the time for truths, for apologies. "I meant I'm sorry I've been so busy trying to be perfect, always racing toward a future, that I didn't...that I haven't really *known* you. And that I've kept so much locked inside me. So much I didn't even realize it must have been difficult for you to know me."

Anne smiled and wiped her own tears. She took a tissue and handed Poppy one. "I'm glad you came back here, Poppy. I'm pissed as to what made you flee Paris and heartbroken for what you thought about your dad, but I am so glad you're here now."

"Wow," Poppy said. "Anne Bergstrom, did you just say *pissed*?"

"Don't be absurd." Her mom tickled her toes and Poppy scrambled them away and out of her mom's reach. "I'm allowed to curse when a monster hurts my daughter."

"Okay," Poppy said, determined to conquer the tears this time. She'd cried enough for one day. But feeling surrounded by love felt extraordinarily awesome.

"Your Rafe seems lovely." Anne picked up her knitting and Poppy watched as her mom's hands flew through the stitches. "He left you some tea in your mug." Sure enough, there was the pretty green travel mug with flowers painted on the side. Poppy pulled the note out from under it.

Poppy, I'm not far. Call me if you need me. Your mom was worried and wanted to sit with you... Did you know you're even beautiful when you cry? Your Rafe.

The flurries twirled in her belly all over again. She smiled and touched the note to her mouth. Sweet, sweet man. *Your Rafe*. How she wanted it to be true.

"I convinced him to let me stay with you while he showed Will his shop. It seems that's as far away from you as he was willing to go. And it felt like he could use a bit of movement."

"How long have they been out there?" Poppy grinned at the thought of Rafe and her stepfather together.

"Oh, for an hour now."

"They've probably already finished an addition to the house," she said and giggled.

"You're probably right," her mom said and laughed with Poppy. "I bet Will's in heaven. He hasn't gotten his hands dirty building anything in years."

Her stepfather had a hugely successful architecture firm in New York, but Poppy couldn't remember ever seeing him work with tools. Maybe it was one more example of her not paying attention.

"Sooo," her mother said. "Your young man is awfully handsome."

"Oh whew, there's the proper Boston heiress I know and love." Poppy rolled her eyes. "Young man is not what I would call Rafe at all." She stretched out her leg and toed her mom's hip again.

"Mm." Anne raised an eyebrow. "Did you miss the part where I said 'awfully handsome?'"

"No, Mom. I didn't miss it at all."

"And I'm right, aren't I?"

"Yes," Poppy said and giggled again. "He sure is."

"He makes you happy." A statement, not a question.

"So, so happy," Poppy whispered. "It almost scares me." She pulled the blanket to her chin.

Anne paused her knitting again. "I think it's time for a bunch of happiness in your life, Poppy."

Poppy allowed her mom's words to swirl inside her.

"Graciella is beautiful, a joyful place for us once a long time ago. Maybe it could be yours again. I'd forgotten how much I loved this town. Maybe I'm good at shoving away the difficult too." Her mom sighed. "Not so hard to come back with Will by my side. It's easier to remember the good times. Have you been by the house?"

"I have," Poppy said. "When I first arrived. It was occupied. But then Rafe and I were there yesterday, and it was empty."

"It's been rented out over the years. The money has gone into an account for you and to pay for upkeep. The previous renters recently ended their lease. Fortuitous, don't you think? All the things you could do with a charming house in a burgeoning downtown full of dreams and hope."

Full of dreams and hope sounded like a rainbow Poppy wanted to climb and ride off into the sunset. Maybe she'd be lucky enough to add one more word to that—love. A noise rumbled through the room and startled them both.

"Oh my God!"

"Was that your stomach?" her mom asked and let out a full laugh.

Poppy couldn't help the smile that burst over her face. Her mom was lovely when she laughed. "I think I'm hungry."

Her mom's face softened into a grin. "You think?"

"Yeah, and you know what else I'd forgotten about this place? How much they all love to cook and eat. Even Rafe's a really good cook." She blushed as soon as she'd said it, remembering how their fondue dinner had ended last night.

Her mom's grin grew wider. "So is Will."

They burst out laughing and Poppy thought laughter had never ever felt so good.

"Thanks for coming, Mom."

"Anytime, my love. I am always here for you. Now, your phone and my phone have been blowing up with texts. You have a lot of people concerned. Let's ease their worry, shall we?"

Poppy nodded.

"Oh, Katie says if we'd like, everyone would love to bring dinner over tonight so they can take care of us."

"That sounds amazing, but the only way I'm letting people come over and visit is if I can get a shower first. Even my shirt is still wet from tears. I can't imagine how puffy my face is."

"You are my beautiful girl, no matter what. But I completely understand. Now scoot. I'll reply to the texts."

Having an uber-efficient mother who enjoyed taking care of all the details wasn't always a negative. Poppy dragged her tired body upstairs, but she did it feeling lighter than she had in years, and she also did it holding a pretty mug of tea and another note to add to her collection.

Chapter Twenty-Three

Poppy's mom and stepdad were nice people, from what Rafe could tell having only spent a bit of time with them, but his lingering concern over Poppy prevented him from being one hundred percent present with them. Showing Will the shop had been a good distraction and Anne had been right — he'd needed to move, be active. Crawling out of his skin with worry wasn't doing him any good. Now Will and Anne were taking a break at the cottage, where they'd be staying, before everyone apparently descended on Rafe's house for dinner under the guise of checking on Poppy. The Brockmans adored her. How could they not? Of course they'd want to check on her.

He climbed the stairs, searching for her. Pausing a moment in the entry to his bathroom, he watched her through the glass shower wall. She wasn't crying anymore. She was singing. He didn't know the song, something about *ain't no love*, and she was a bit off key, but it was the prettiest sound to ever hit his ears. Not to mention how beautiful she was standing there naked, eyes closed, head flung back under the spray of water, rinsing soapy bubbles from her hair, all dark and sleek when it was wet. A water goddess, a fairy, a lover, all these things he never imagined for himself.

Rafe let the worry surge out of him in one long breath as he stripped his clothes and followed his beauty into the shower. "Hey," he said gently so as not to startle her. He ran his hands through her hair, helping the soap rinse away as her body melted against his. And when she faced him and opened her eyes, he felt it, the sun burning through his chest.

"Hi." She studied his face. "Are you okay?"

"Me?" Rafe put his hands on her hips, drawing her near so their bodies connected, so he could feel the warmth of her sunshine all through him.

She wrapped her arms around his neck. "I was kind of a mess when you found me."

"I don't mind your mess."

She sighed into his body and her smile blinded him. "You take such good care of me."

The feel of her fingers brushing against his brow was almost more than he could handle. That combined with the way she saw into his depths and was fascinated anyway. Her mouth parted in wonder, in invitation. Lush, wet body pressed against his. He kissed her then. What else was he meant to do with her offering but worship.

Rafe gripped her ass and hauled her up. Poppy whimpered and clasped her legs around him, returning his kiss with a frenzy that matched the beat inside his chest. Marking each other, making sure the message was clear, the intention, the need, the desire. She tangled her tongue with his, held his head to her and ravaged him, sucking and tasting while moving her body into his.

"Needed to be with you," Rafe panted and moved her against the shower wall.

"Me too," she said.

He kissed her words away, swallowed her goodness. He ripped his mouth away, rested his forehead against hers. "Need to be inside you. Is that...is that okay?" God, his need to bind them together was fierce, but he'd never betray her desires or what she needed in the moment.

"Yes, now, Rafe."

Poppy circled his dick with those magnificent hands of hers, guiding him to her entrance. It was a thing of beauty, her taking what she wanted, arched against him, seeking the connection as desperately as he did. But then his ache overtook him, and he gripped her hands, moved them above her head and thrust into her in one motion.

Fuck, the emotions swirling around them, and her wet warmth was enough to make him come. He stilled, breathed in all the sensations, barely held himself in check trying to make this moment last as long as it could. All these moments he tried to speak to her with his body.

"Oh, thank goodness for strong leg muscles," she said and grinned, her face dripping and flushed, smile lazy with desire. She smoothed her hands over his chest.

How could she tease at a moment like this? But she wasn't wrong. All those times growing up kids had made fun of his size washed down the drain. Now he felt powerful, holding them both, thrusting into her, hearing and feeling her moans. The way her feet dug into his butt. He soaked up the trust she placed in him to hold her, make things good for her. He nipped at her cheeky mouth, sucked that gorgeous plump lower lip in and poured everything he had into the kiss while he rubbed his body against hers.

Her whimpers and moans increased, and he knew she was close.

"Rafe," she pleaded.

He picked up the pace, let go of her arms and wrapped his around her so he wouldn't hurt her against the wall.

"Oh, God, I'm going to—I'm so close I..." Poppy sucked on his neck as her entire body clamped around his.

He couldn't make it last. It was now. Rafe exploded into her as she shattered around him, pulling him into her sacred place. Their crash was electric. And he felt it then, her sunshine bursting all around him, pumping him for all he was worth.

"Wow." Poppy's voice was a hush between them.

Rafe couldn't speak at all. He squeezed her to him. They were still connected. *Wow* was right. Slowly he pulled out of her and set her on her feet under the spray, catching her when she wobbled. Carefully with the one brain cell he had in working order because she had literally blown his mind, he soaped a sponge and cleaned their bodies. Then Rafe turned the water off and stepped them both out of the shower. He grabbed a large towel and wrapped it around Poppy. Tagged another one for himself and tugged her into him.

They didn't speak for a few minutes, just stared at each other. Rafe took her hand and put it over his chest, holding it there with his own. *I love you*, he wanted to say, wanted the words to come out easy and clear.

Poppy smiled and put her other hand on his cheek, as if she knew. Maybe. Did she feel the same?

"What?" she whispered.

Was she giving him permission? One of her gorgeous green eyes was slightly bigger than the other and some of her freckles spilled over onto her lip. A scar graced her chin, from what, he didn't know. But he wanted to, he wanted to listen to all her stories. Maybe his speech didn't need to be impeccable. She seemed not to mind his stutter whenever it crashed the party.

"I am falling..." Rafe took a deep breath. *Slow and steady, slow and steady.* "I am falling in love wi-with you, Poppy." Witnessing her eyes grow wide then soften was a sight Rafe would never forget.

Then she snuggled closer, wrapped both arms around him, never breaking eye contact and whispered against his lips, "I am falling madly in love with you too, Rafe."

Rafe sighed then, and laughed. He picked her up and twirled her around.

"I've never heard you laugh."

"Mm." *Not much reason to before. Before you came into my life and shocked me back to the land of joy and happiness.*

"I can't believe it. This." She gestured between them. "It hasn't been very long, but my heart recognizes yours," she whispered.

Rafe understood the need for whispers. This love was still something precious to keep between each other. "Mine too," he whispered, and placed a soft kiss on her lips.

"I wish we could stay in our happy bubble here, the two of us."

Her stomach grumbled between them. "Better let them feed you. They, they're worried. Want to make sure you're okay."

"Yeah." She pouted. "I am hungry. Could we come back here when they leave? We just said I love you to each other. I've never said that before and it feels precious. I want to say it again and savor it with you."

She'd reached in and stolen the words from inside him. "I promise."

Chapter Twenty-Four

The aroma was intoxicating. Garlic and wine, an amazing combination that drew Poppy to the top of the stairs. She'd heard people arriving and had finished adding a brush of makeup to her happy but still tired face. Part of her really did want to stay upstairs with Rafe for the next hundred years, but hunger and the desire to ease everyone's concern urged her into the fray. She also secretly delighted in having company in Rafe's house. Their first official gathering together. She chewed on her lip. Could they call it their first gathering if she hadn't contributed anything to it?

"Hey."

"Poppy." A chorus of voices and smiles hit her. But it was the scents coming from the kitchen that had her drooling.

"What in the heck smells so good?"

Rafe's gaze seared into her from across the room. He was standing in the corner beside Will. He had his arms crossed and his mouth tipped up at the corner and she nearly melted into a puddle of goo. How in the world could he tease her and make her hot with one almost grin from all the way over there? She knew her own smile in return was full and loopy and she didn't care. She was in love, and, holy cow, she was loved. Rafe loved *her*, Poppy. Unbelievable. Not to mention all these people had dropped everything two days before Christmas to come be with her.

"Lily and Turner made platters full of shrimp scampi, dripping in garlic butter and wine," her mom said. "There's pasta on the side. Katie brought homemade baguettes, Everyone brought something. Cass baked brownies—"

"Brownies!" Emi, one of Luca and Gabby's girls, yelled, and everyone laughed.

"And Will and I brought the wine," her mom finished.

Suddenly, with all the stares aimed at her, shyness overcame Poppy. Rafe was at her side in an instant, all quiet confidence, and she leaned right into him for a hug. His warmth surrounded her.

"All of this for me?" she whispered.

"They love you."

Before she could be overcome by emotion again, chatter and noise resumed, her aunt came over and Rafe handed Poppy off for a different, no less wonderful kind of hug.

"You doing okay, honey?" Katie asked.

"Better." Poppy squeezed back, welcoming this contact with her aunt, letting the good memories sweep over her.

"Hey, lady." Lily was beside her next. "Glass of wine?"

Poppy took the glass and gave Lily a soft side hug, gazing down at the tiny newborn Lily had wrapped up in a baby sling. "What are you doing here? Congratulations, new mama." Poppy brushed her hand over baby Theo's head.

Lily glowed. "I feel like we have a million family members and friends helping us. We're so lucky. And I've missed you. Seems like lots has happened since you got here?" Her grin was huge. "I need all the gossip, and any excuse for me to make my scampi is a good one. Hopefully you'll love it so much we'll lure you into staying. It worked on Miranda."

Miranda laughed. She held her own sleeping baby on her shoulder and was gently patting her butt. "It was more than the scampi."

"Yes, but it was all part of the plan—we needed more people to love, and you needed a family," Lily said.

Poppy swallowed back more tears at the simplicity but rawness of Lily's words, as if it really was that easy. That all one had to do was decide they wanted love and a family, then one could so easily discover it.

Turner pulled an enormous sheet pan of shrimp out of the oven, stirring the butter and garlic sauce all over it. The aroma almost had Poppy fainting again. She hadn't eaten all day. And it had been the longest day ever in many ways. The front door opened, and Adam walked in with Luca and Jake.

"Oh, it's time," Lily squealed and made her way to Turner who planted a gentle kiss on her mouth then on Theo's head.

Gosh, I adore this group of people.

"Everybody back up," Luca Rossi, Gabby's fiancé, yelled.

"What's going on?" her mom asked.

"I have no idea," Poppy said.

"I love surprises," Miranda said and came to stand by them.

The guys all wrestled a gorgeous long dining room table inside. Rafe stiffened next to her. She reached for his hand.

"Surprise!" Lily yelled. "We made you a table, Rafe."

Poppy leaned her body into Rafe's.

"I...what? Why?" he said.

"Duh," Lily said softly. "Because you're family. And you can't have family dinners without a dining room table. We've been working on it for a while, got distracted with wedding stuff."

Rafe took a tiny step forward, then stopped. He looked down at Poppy and she smiled and nudged him forward. There was no stopping the tears this time, not with Lily's words, not with the vulnerability and hope in Rafe's expression, and certainly not when Rafe quietly, reverently ran his hands over the fine planks of wood, as if this simple table was the most beautiful thing he'd ever seen. She felt that way when he touched her, and it melted her heart all over in this moment.

"Benches too, for now," Lily continued. "But you can add chairs later if you want."

Javier was there by Rafe's side. "We know you could have built your own, but we weren't sure you'd ever get around to it. If you don't like it—"

"I like it," Rafe said, a catch in his voice.

"Wow," her mom whispered next to Poppy. Will stood behind Anne with his arms around her, a huge smile on his face.

"Yeah," Poppy said.

Willow climbed onto one of the benches and put her hands on the table. "Let's eat," she said. "I'm hungry."

Poppy laughed. "Me too!"

Then, as if they'd done this a million times, in this room, the table was set with food and wine. Highchairs were full of babies. People sat, kids and adults all mixed together, and Katie raised her glass.

"To family, to sharing great meals together and to love."

Poppy clinked glasses and sipped her wine before she cried into her food. Rafe sat beside her, still looking shell-shocked. He held her hand on his lap while people passed the food.

"Okay?" Poppy asked.

He gave her the most brilliant smile and nodded.

Poppy leaned over, kissed his cheek and whispered, "They love you too." His eyes sparked at that. "Now you have to let go of my hand so I can eat this delicious food before I face-plant into it."

He gave one last squeeze to her fingers and let her go. And Poppy ate the most mouthwatering scampi of her life, sopped up garlic butter sauce with fresh bread and drank the best Chardonnay she'd ever had, surrounded by family, surrounded by love. When she was finished and her napkin was on her plate and people were telling stories and the twins were asleep on Adam's shoulders, and Cruz was walking around the room with a tired baby in his arms, while Willow, Emi and Tess drew at the window table, with laughter and voices and the cozy heat of the fire, Rafe took her hand back with his and held it close to him.

And Poppy realized a person could fall in love more than once with a person, with a place. Something powerful settled deep inside her. Here was where she wanted to be, in this house, with this man, surrounded by family and friends who loved them. And so she did, fall in love all over again with the people, with the place and with her new soulmate.

* * * *

"Goodnight, Mom." Poppy gave one last hug before Anne and Will made their way to the cottage.

Rafe closed the door to her parents, slipped his hand into Poppy's, led her upstairs and made good on his promise, stripping them naked and snuggling them into their cocoon of love. He was gentle and slow, worshipping her body with his hands and his lips while she floated on a plane of happy exhausted and let him make love to her while the stars twinkled outside and inside she was very warm indeed.

Chapter Twenty-Five

"It feels so weird, seeing it empty," Poppy said. Echoes fanned out around her as she walked across the living room to the small kitchen.

"It sure does." Her mom stood in the doorway of their old house, now Poppy's house on Main Street.

Bare wood floors, no curtains on the windows. Walls that needed new paint. It all felt old, in a well-loved, but lonely way. *Perhaps the loneliness comes with seeing it empty, as if its heartbeat departed with the last renters.*

"You okay?" she asked her mom, who hadn't come any farther into the house. It was only the two of them. Will and Rafe had dropped them off and headed toward the hardware store. The four of them had started this beautiful Christmas Eve morning with breakfast together. Then they'd nearly laughed themselves silly picking out a Christmas tree for Rafe's house. Now she and her mom were taking a weird walk down memory lane.

Anne started forward slowly, taking it all in. "I am. It's bringing back a lot of memories. I loved this little house so much when we bought it. It didn't cost much. We thought it did at the time since we were young. The neighborhood was a little ragged, but we saw so much potential. Your dad and I refinished the floors ourselves, and painted, different colors than they have now." Anne ran her fingers over the fireplace mantel.

"What, uh…" Poppy paused, wanting to ask, but worried about bringing up past wounds. It was time, though, now that her past had been busted wide open. "What happened between you and dad?"

Anne closed her eyes and let out a long breath.

"I remember you guys fighting. I mean, I didn't remember it until recently. There was this night when you shut him out and went to bed crying. It wasn't the only night that happened, was it?"

"No, honey. It wasn't. He'd started to do well with his painting, and I'd been working so hard to keep a roof over our heads so he could do his art. I knew it would take off. I knew people would love it. And they did. Unfortunately, all the acclaim came with a lot of pressure. Your dad started drinking and going to parties, even if I couldn't go with him. Then he was traveling so much and we started to grow apart, little by little. It's hard to be separated, especially with a child in the picture. But it was the drinking that broke us. When he wouldn't get help for it, I didn't know how to move forward. It broke my trust, my self-esteem, my heart."

"He cheated on you?" Poppy wasn't as shocked as she might have been even a few weeks ago with the memories that had been playing through her mind.

"It's okay, Mom. You can tell me if you want. I can handle it."

"No, honey. But he kept making awful choices, prioritizing alcohol over...over us. I didn't have anything left to give after a while. So, I filed for divorce, packed you and me up and returned to Boston. A week later he died. It was horrible."

"I think I remember the drinking, Mom. Little by little memories are sneaking back in."

"I'm so sorry, honey. I'm so sorry about all of it. I'm here if you want to talk more about any of it. Or if you think you need a counselor, I support you."

Poppy wrapped her mom up in an enormous hug. "Thank you," she whispered. "It does help to talk about it, in sort of a painful way. If that makes any sense."

Her mother held her away and looked at Poppy. "I understand."

"Grandpa died around then too."

"Yes, and things were so difficult and sad for a while."

"Until you met Will?" Poppy was drawn to this conversation, even though it shed not-so-great light on her dad. Talking, really talking with her mom was like discovering a gem in the sand. Precious and stunning. It had been there, all these truths and this connection, but it had been buried for so long, hidden from them all together.

Her mom laughed and the smile she gave brightened the entire empty house and eased the sad feeling in Poppy's chest. "Not exactly. I mean yes, falling in love with Will was wonderful, but that wasn't until a few years later. After your grandfather died, I went back to school and found I really loved design. You were doing well, and the clouds lifted. But Will was, *is* wonderful. He brought so much light into our life I was almost afraid at first to grab onto it."

"Good thing he's super stubborn," Poppy said, and her mom laughed again.

They peeked into the bedrooms and small bathroom at the back of the house and climbed up to see the loft area.

"When you know, you know. I felt so safe around Will, but also excited. My pulse jumped for joy every time he was around." Poppy's mom nudged her as they stared at the low light coming through the tall window in the loft. "I think you understand exactly what I'm saying. Am I right?"

Poppy didn't bother to hide the smile or the blush that bloomed on her cheeks. "I've never met anyone like Rafe before. He's so good to me. Exactly what you said, safe but giddy, and like he's exactly where I belong. Belonging is something I didn't realize I'd been searching for until I arrived back here in Graciella."

"Oh, honey. I'm so sorry."

"Maybe we should quit apologizing. It's not anyone's fault. I kept shields around myself. I...I was closed off to anything good, within myself or connecting with others. It was all about how well I did at school and at my jobs, all these external things. And as horrible as my experience in Paris was, as broken as I was when I came here, I got lucky that Rafe was who witnessed my vulnerability. Does that make sense?"

"Yes," Anne said. "You were open to love and love walked in."

"Exactly. And I don't mean he can fix all of my broken parts, but being loved and loving someone can be healing in its own way." Poppy pressed her hand against her heart.

Her mom nodded and made her way back down the stairs. "He's quiet," Anne said.

Whew, he definitely communicates in his own way.

"But I see the way his eyes follow you and the way he treats you, Poppy. How he treats everyone around him. That was a nice thing they did, making him a table, insisting that he belongs here. It says a lot about how they feel about him. And Will says his craftsmanship is the best he's ever seen."

"Well, he does do amazing work with his hands."

Anne's loud laughter boomed through the house. "So, my dear, what are you going to do with this place?"

Poppy closed her eyes and imagined. She had an artist's eye, from both her parents. She'd grown up surrounded by her mother's interior design projects. It was practically in her blood. But she didn't see this house as the place she wanted to live. When she tried to imagine home these days, it was Rafe's house in her mind, or rather Rafe. Wherever he was felt like belonging. The little window-filled nook, as though he'd built it for the two of them, the fireplaces, the scent of wood on his skin when he came in from working in his shop, his bed, his long johns.

Her sigh was deliriously happy. "I'm not sure. It's still sinking in that it belongs to me. But it feels wonderful owning a piece of Graciella. Even though I shut out a lot of the bad memories, I loved this place."

"You know, honey..." Anne twirled around the front room, gazed left and right out of the front window. "This could make a great shop. You've always wanted your own."

Oh. That thought burst into her heart. She'd never in her wildest dreams imagined being this young and attaining that goal. First was supposed to come the long tenure, or indentured servitude, at the Paris fashion houses. Next, getting to spotlight her own collection at some point. And finally, beginning to make a name for herself. Could she really have her own clothing shop at this stage in her life?

"You're ready, honey. I think you've been ready for a while, and unfortunately I pushed you in the direction of more study, always more study." Anne approached her and took Poppy's face in her hands. "But your designs have been golden for a long time, love. And your business knowledge has always been excellent. It's definitely your time to shine."

"I've been dreaming of my own shop," Poppy whispered.

"Yes, you have," Anne said.

Poppy reached inside her heart and opened her vision. It could be perfect in this charming old house. "A mixture of new designers, some used clothes, all sizes and shapes."

"Vintage, darling. Not used."

"Hah!" Poppy laughed. "We'll call it vintage for your delicate sensibilities."

"Thank you. Now let's go find the boys and get Donny's Pizza. I've been missing it for over seventeen years."

* * * *

"This is one of the coolest hardware stores I've ever seen." Will gushed over the space.

Rafe understood how Moreno Hardware could transform an award-winning, perhaps stuffy architect from the East Coast into a laid-back surfer type, full of awe for the next big wave. Under Lily Brockman's hovering eye, her parents' old hardware shop had been restored a few years ago. It *was* one cool place.

High ceilings, nooks and crannies, new-made-to-look-old wooden shelves and bins. The enormous apothecary's cabinet behind the register. One could say it was designed for style as well as function. Rafe sensed the ghosts whenever he walked in. They hovered from another era, not angry, merely interested in the people now traipsing the space. He'd never in his life felt a hardware store had a sacred presence, but this one sure did.

He wanted to find handles for the drawers and cupboards of the cabinet he was building for Poppy. Antiques to give it character, something special like her. The old brass ones would go well with the walnut. He also grabbed lights for the tree and a tree stand since he'd never owned either before. He also didn't have any ornaments. *Wonder what Poppy will say when I tell her that?* He hadn't had the guts to admit it when they were shopping for a tree. He thought maybe they could decorate with lights this year and build on their decorations together year after year. That thought made him smile.

Will had suggested they separate when they'd been on their way into town, which saved Rafe having to sneak into the hardware store without Poppy tagging along. He wanted the cabinet to be a surprise. He hadn't even shown it to Will last night when Anne had shooed them out of the house. He'd shown him the bookshelves and his designs for the new wells, but the cabinet had stayed under its cloth. He wanted Poppy to see it first, before anyone else.

Will was pocketing his phone when he approached Rafe at the register. His grin was wide as they walked to meet the ladies for pizza. "It's a good place you've found here, Rafe. Didn't have a clue what to expect, but the mixture of retail and houses, the restoration of many of the old buildings... They've made it charming as well as a good place to live."

Rafe was listening until he caught sight of Poppy and her mother waiting for them on the sidewalk. Instantly all his attention was drawn to her. Every other thought or conversation blew away on the wind. When she turned and smiled at him, his heart did that funny thing again where it started thumping against his ribcage, trying to get to her. He leaned in for a soft kiss, pulling away before he dragged her behind one of the buildings to ravish her against the wall while the snow fell around them.

"Shall we?" Will held the door open and the delicious humid scents drew them inside. Rafe would have to wait till later to get her naked. He embraced his patience, a skill that had always served him well.

"Table for four," Will said, and a waitress led them to a booth. It was good Poppy held on to his hand because he found, as he focused on not ravishing her, any other decisions his brain might have to make took a lot of effort.

"Look at you two." Donny slapped Rafe on the shoulder and winked. "Snuggling close together. Good for you, eh. And..." He turned toward Will and Anne. "Goodness, if it isn't Annie O'Brien in the flesh." Donny tugged from the booth and gave her a hug.

"It's Anne Bergstrom now. This is my husband, Will Bergstrom. Will, Donny, creator of the best pizza in the West."

"I can't believe it. It's been how many years?" Donny whisked a tear from his cheek.

"Almost eighteen," Anne said.

"First Poppy, and now you." Don wiped his face with his towel. "Anne was the best waitress I ever had," he said to Poppy. "Too bad the boys kept hitting on her."

"You were a waitress?" Poppy laughed and Rafe settled beside her.

Her emotions vibrated through her touch, and her laugh was one of his favorite things. He'd been worried about her going to see her old house, but she'd assured him it would be fine. If he had to gauge her mood right now, it was light and happy.

"I was," Anne bragged. "A darn good one. Oh gosh it was so fun. I'm so glad you're still here, Donny."

"Ah well, we had a rough couple of years there where we had to close our doors. People were skedaddling out of Graciella as fast as they could. Wasn't much reason to stay when TD started buying all the properties. Mean old bastard. I'm not ashamed to say I cheered when they buried his dark soul. Now things are hoppin'." He smacked the table with his towel. "You moving back?"

"No." Anne laughed. "We're just visiting. Poppy might stick around."

Will she? Could this really be a place she'd want to stay? He'd never been in love before, but it felt like everything suddenly — air and water and life.

"You couldn't pick a nicer town, darlin'. Now let me get wine for the table. A bottle of my best red on the house."

"Oh, I almost forgot, Poppy," Will said. "I got a call from Renee Laurent."

"*The* Renee Laurent?" Poppy asked in a hushed whisper. "Only one of the greatest designers in French history!"

Will nodded. "Our families are acquainted. I haven't spoken to her in years, but I called her immediately when I found out what happened to you, Poppy. She has a job waiting for you in Paris if you want. I can guarantee you will be treated with respect. And..." Will winked. "She loved your latest designs."

"What?" Anne and Poppy spoke at the same time.

"You sent her my designs?" Poppy asked.

"Of course I did. Your talent deserves recognition, honey. I could never replace your real father, but I've loved you as my own daughter since you came into my life. I had to do something. And short of beating the crap out of your old boss, I called in a favor, for family."

"A job with Renee Laurent? That's unheard of." Poppy's hushed awe stabbed Rafe in the gut. His heart fell with a thud, all the wind knocked right out of him. *She has a job waiting for her in Paris. A dream job.*

"I...I...don't know what to say." Poppy's voice was wobbly.

Instinctively Rafe reached out and wiped the tear from her cheek. Her smile, that damn brilliant smile of hers was killing him now. "Thank you so much, Will. I... That means so much to me, but I—"

"Garlic knots and wine all around," Donny interrupted them with a tray of wineglasses and the favorite garlic bread. Don held up his own glass and made a toast, "To new beginnings."

Glasses clinked. Rafe's body followed along, while inside his, heart buried itself under the pain of not being enough, all over again.

Chapter Twenty-Six

"Goodnight, darling. You've got a lot to ponder. This might sound foreign coming from me, but go with what's in your heart. It's always the riskiest, and it requires the utmost bravery, putting yourself out there. But it's also what will bring you the most happiness."

Poppy paid close attention to her mother's words. They were a blessing because Poppy already knew what she wanted, what she was going to do. At least she had until they'd left the pizza parlor. Or maybe things had turned weird when they were eating. Poppy couldn't pinpoint the moment Rafe had draped a cold shield around himself. Even now, in his warm house with the fire going, the chill radiated from him.

"Goodnight, Rafe. Thank you for a lovely day." Anne and Will shut the door and took all the rest of the warmth with them.

Silence wasn't Poppy's friend now. It pulsed around them, weighed down the air, nearly sucked the breath from her. She and Rafe stood fifteen feet apart. They may as well have been on separate planets.

"I'm… I-I need to-to…work," Rafe said, without looking at her.

Then he strode out through the back door and left her standing alone in his house, without a mug of tea, without a note, without any clue as to what had happened since they'd left town. *Wait! It's Christmas Eve. We got a tree! What happened?* The tears started then and she couldn't stop them. Since she'd returned to this beautiful place, each day had been a blessing, a new start with wondrous things happening all around her.

And for the first time in her life, she was fully in love with another human. That was the star on the top of the tree, the gem of these last few weeks. But, having spent so much time with Rafe, she could read his body language now, so skilled was he with communicating that way. His touch, a smile, the way he growled when he ravished her mouth, the reverence he paid to her body, how careful he'd been with her, how he listened. And for the last hour or so, he'd held himself completely away from her, body and soul. He'd even carefully snaked his hand away from hers at Donny's when she'd tried to connect them.

Maybe the afternoon had been too much for him with her parents. Maybe he needed a break and couldn't communicate it to her. She made up things to soothe her own bruised soul. *Why does it feel like something monumental is going on instead? And why was he so cold? Why did he walk away? We said we love each other.* Poppy paced the gorgeous wood floors Rafe had sanded by hand. *Perfect, stupid, stubborn hands.* Irritation and hurt battled with her confusion.

She stopped and took a deep breath. There was a lovely spot in front of the enormous front window for the tree. At least she thought it was. That was what they were supposed to be doing now, putting up the tree, enjoying each other's company, gazing into each other's eyes, kissing, loving.

"Dammit." Poppy huffed and grabbed her jacket. *I can bring the damn tree in by myself.* She pulled open the front door just as Cass was about to knock.

"Hi...uh...are you okay?" Cass, Gabby, Vivianna, Katie, Miranda and Lily with her newborn snuggled in a baby carrier against her chest, stood on Rafe's front porch.

"I'm...I'm..."

"You're crying," Katie said and pushed her way in.

Wrapped up in her aunt's arms, Poppy let the rogue tears fall despite being more angry than upset at the moment. *Angry tears are new, that's for sure.* "I'm sorry," Poppy said. "I... Rafe... And he... I don't even know what happened, but he... Things were lovely. We even bought a tree. But something happened and he's gone all cold and distant. And I want to stay here and be with him, in this beautiful house on this farm, surrounded by all of you, by my family and new friends. I want to fill his life with warmth and joy and memories, like he's already done for me."

"It's okay to be upset when someone hurts you, even if they don't mean to hurt you," Katie said.

"He didn't even do anything, really," she said and rubbed her eyes. "I mean, how ridiculous is that. He did *nothing*. But that hurts."

"Well," Katie said. "You may have picked a wonderful man to fall in love with, but you also picked the most stubborn man I've ever met."

"And that's saying a ton," Lily said. "Since she has three extremely stubborn sons. Jesus, Rafe would still be building this house all by himself stick by stick if we hadn't finally barged in and helped him."

"That's right." Cass laughed. "He doesn't want to bother anyone. So he wasn't going to ask Lily and her company, or any of us to help him. And remember when they were digging for that well when he first came to Graciella?"

"Oh, shoot." Now her aunt was laughing. "I thought he was going to slice his own skin open and pour his blood right into the work he was that determined to wring water from our damaged dry land. We couldn't even drag him home to eat."

Poppy slumped onto the sofa. "That all sounds like his ridiculous, fabulous self, but this feels different in that he pulled away. I want him to put all that focus and energy into working things out with me. Whatever the heck it even is we need to work out."

"Hm," Vivianna said quietly. Poppy had liked Vivianna from the first time she met her. She was quiet like Rafe. "I remember when Jake tried to push me away, when he thought he was doing something for my own good."

"Oh, Lord, these men and our own good," Miranda said.

Vivianna laughed. "Right." She turned back to Poppy "Maybe he's pulling away to protect himself from getting hurt. I get that. Loving a person and wondering if they feel the same, *want* the same things is frightening. Did something scare him?"

"Ugh." Poppy flung her head back. "I don't know. We had a great day in town, all four of us. My mom and I separated from the guys. Then we all met up for pizza and…" She sat up. "Oh boy, I might be able to guess. Will has a contact in the Paris fashion world who offered me a job. in Paris."

"Ahh," Katie said. "I bet you're right. That poor man hasn't ever had anyone care enough about him to want to keep him."

"Except us," Miranda said.

"What?" *How can that be?* Poppy was shocked. He was kind, thoughtful, sexy as heck, talented. He was hers was what he was, stubborn ridiculous silence and all.

"Maybe he needs a push," Lily suggested. "I think you should be totally honest and tell him exactly what you want."

Poppy sighed. She could do that. She'd love to know exactly what he wanted too. *Would it work?* He wasn't the easiest man to get to open up. She squeezed Lily's hand. "What are you all doing here anyway? I love that you can stop by one another's houses all the time, but it's Christmas Eve. Don't you have a million things to do?"

"It's just a quick visit," Miranda said. "We all thought you and Rafe could use a few Christmas decorations so we each picked a few ornaments to give you, for your first Christmas together."

"Oh." Poppy was crying again. "I love that so much." She brushed her tears away. "I really need to go talk to Rafe."

"Want us to help you get your tree inside first?" Gabby asked. "Help shove that stubborn man into a life with you."

"I would love that," Poppy said.

It took them only a few minutes to heave the seven-foot-tall tree inside, and Cass was amazing at getting it into the tree stand. As soon as they'd watered it, the scent of fresh pine filled her senses, cleansing, clearing. The physical movement did her good. The hugs did her better as her family said their goodbyes, and now Poppy felt ready to take on the fortress of Rafe Holmes.

* * * *

"What's going on?"

Poppy and the wind blew open the shop door and swooshed into his space. She'd been invading his space since she'd arrived, with her exploded suitcase, goldilocksing her way into his bed. Her buttons and threads, her wild hair, lusty laugh and fairy eyes, her scent, the way she'd reached in and excavated his heart.

Rafe tossed his sanding block away and tried to brace himself against the workbench. His hands shook. An anvil pressed against his chest. He'd barely gotten anything done since he'd stormed out here. Unable to safely hold his drill or the wood against the planer, sanding by hand had been the only thing he'd been capable of, barely. *Is this how it's going to be now, or when she leaves? Me unable to work, to function, to breathe?*

"Rafe? Please talk to me."

"Nothing. I-I-I'm working." His words were coated in sludge, each one more painful than the last to get out.

"Don't...don't lie to me, please, Rafe. You've been pulling away, distant since lunch. Something happened. You...you've been holding my hand. Holding it close, especially since we said I love you."

He studied his pathetic hands, lost now without her. She placed her hand on his arm and Rafe let out a deep breath. Her warmth, she'd take that with her too. He pulled away, watched her flinch at the movement. A harsh, pained expression swam across her face. That was the last thing he wanted to do, cause her pain.

"I'm pretty certain I didn't do anything wrong. I mean, something's wrong, but instead of telling me, you walked away. I deserve more than that, from people, from *you*."

Fuck. She was right. He'd done what he was expecting her to do, walk away without any explanation.

"But then Aunt Katie and all the ladies stopped by and helped me understand maybe you're afraid, that you, that you think Paris is what I want —"

"I can't...can't make you stay, ph-physically." The pounding in his head was in his heart now, angry, fierce, mocking him. *Afraid?* Maybe he was. To have such beauty and light in his life then have it all swept away so quickly. He wasn't sure he could withstand it. "I-I-I...fuck! I have to let you go ba-back there," he yelled. "If that's what you want. I can't ma-ma-make you stay."

Poppy shook her head. He reached out his arm, wanted to smooth away her tears, let it drop. His own tears fell then, making his face wet.

"No, you can't make someone stay. You can't make me stay, but that doesn't matter because I *want* to." She stepped into him.

"I-I...want you, to want me enough to-to-to make that choice. Wait..." The storm in his vision cleared. He took a tentative step closer. "Did you say...?"

She nodded as more tears fell, but it was her gorgeous smile that finally cracked through the blustering tornado and made some sense. He grabbed her and kissed her, quenching the ache in his heart with her.

"Yes, Rafe. I want to be here with you, in Graciella, on the farm, in your house…if you'll have me. I want to build a life with you. I feel incredible with you. I love the way you care for me, the little notes, how you treat my body and my emotions. No one's ever handled me like I'm precious inside and out." She ran her fingers along his cheek, gently touched his lips. "You're precious too. Now tell me, however you can, what do you want?"

"Stay here with me and be mine, let me be yours." The words flew out of his mouth immediately.

"Yes." She nodded. She cupped his face and kissed him. Rafe hugged her and gave a shout. She was laughing and crying with him. "I want to be yours, Rafe. And I want you to be mine."

"I love you. I'm sorry I-I…got scared." She deserved the full truth, she deserved to hear him say how he felt. "You chase away my-my-my darkness. It's blinding how beautiful you are."

"I'm a mess." She gave him a loopy smile and brushed sawdust off his cheek.

"I like your mess. Let me feed you and kiss you and si-sit next to you in our nook I swear I built with you in mind. Let me watch you sew. Let me ca-carry you to bed when you've crashed from exhaustion. Then let me strip you down and worship you."

"That's the best life I could imagine, Rafe, making something magical with you."

He kissed her, making a silent promise to give her exactly that, the best life she could imagine.

"Oh, this is so handsome, Rafe. What is it?" Without letting go of him, Poppy gently caressed the cabinet he'd been working on.

"It's for you, both of these." He gestured toward the table. "A sew-sewing table and a place" — he opened one of the cabinet drawers — "for stuff."

"For me?" Poppy sucked in her breath and stared.

When she didn't say anything right away, he started to worry. Until she turned and fell right into him.

"You started falling in love right away too, didn't you?" Her voice was slightly muffled, but he understood the words, the meaning.

"Yes," he said. He picked her up and held her to him, wrapped them together in their love.

"I can't believe you…I can't believe you did this for me." She wiped off a tear and glanced at the furniture.

"You can always… I mean I like it when you sew at the corner table. But in case you, I thought if you wanted more room… I wanted you to have… something extra-extraordinary. Like you."

"Wow." She grinned. "So, are you going to stay out here and work, or are you going to come in and help me decorate our first Christmas tree?"

"Tree," he said. "Then more kissing." He rested his lips against hers. "Best Christmas ever."

"How can you tell already?" Poppy took his hand and led him outside and across the yard, the lights from the house guiding them. It was snowing again, huge flakes floating gently around them.

"Because I got you, the best…best present ever." Rafe twirled her back into his arms, right where she belonged. He burned for her.

"Rafe?" He loved her voice when it got all husky with need. This time when he kissed her, he lifted her. She wrapped her legs around him and melted into him.

"Tree can wait," he whispered as he carried her inside and upstairs to his bed.

She stripped out of her clothes, tossing her jeans across the room and laughing as he swept her up and fell with her onto the bed. "Want a fire?" he asked in between kisses.

"No." She wrapped her arms and legs around him. "I'm warm enough with you. I'm…" She molded her body against his. "So needy for you, Rafe."

God, she was his flame. Her cheeks and chest bloomed that rosy flush as he dragged his lips over her skin, eliciting moans and gasps from her, drawing out her pleasure. "I feel it too." His cock was nestled right between her thighs, surrounded by her heat. He teased at the entrance.

"Yes, please," she cried and rubbed her body against his.

He cupped one breast and brought it to his mouth, teased at her nipple and felt power surge through him at her moaning response.

"Rafe, hurry…inside me."

He didn't waste another second being separated. With one thrust, he seated himself deep, watched her body bow up at his invasion, felt his heart stutter at the smile that spread over her face. She brought his head to hers and kissed him, again and again. He barely moved, let her tight wet heat clasp around him. With each pulse of her body, she pulled him in deeper. With each arch upward, she drew around him tighter. A fuse sparked along his spine, coiling inside him.

It was the sweetest torture he'd ever experienced, seeing her find her own pleasure, take what she wanted from him. He buried his head in her neck and sucked on the delicate sensitive spot he'd discovered she loved. Dragging one of his hands down, he worked it between their bodies to find her clit and play with it how she liked it, slow and teasing, rubbing his thumb against it until she cried out and came around him in a show of fireworks so gorgeous it was blinding.

Only then did he start moving, pulling out and driving his body back in, harder and faster, seeking all her delights as she shuddered around him. His own release hit him like an explosion, breaking him apart in her arms, surrounded by his love.

Chapter Twenty-Seven

"I love our perfect tree," Poppy said and sighed as she tucked one more fabric bow she'd made onto a branch.

"It's ridiculous." Rafe sat on the couch. His words flowed easily. Maybe his body was too tired to care. A night full of intense lovemaking had emptied his brain of all worries. He'd built a fire after their first round last night, and they'd snuggled and talked long into the night. Rafe had found talking while being naked next to Poppy and having her hands drift over his skin was now one of his favorite things. Their intimate conversations kept leading to more sex, more her, more of them connecting on every level.

It was now afternoon on Christmas Day and the air buzzed with joy. He'd credit Poppy with all of it. So many Christmases as a child he'd been disappointed, not because of presents or decorations, but because he'd been left alone or with neighbors while his mother was chasing his dad. He hadn't lied last night when he'd said this was the best Christmas ever. It was, and he was going to enjoy every minute of it with her.

"It's beautiful." She pouted, standing in front of the enormous tree they'd decorated with lights and the few ornaments the Brockmans and friends had dropped off.

They'd made brunch with her parents this morning and now they were alone again. He loved being alone with her. He tugged her by the waist so she fell onto his lap, giggling as she did it. She situated herself, wrapped her arms around him and kissed him.

"Hi," she whispered. "Being in love is amazing, isn't it?"

He smiled and nodded before he flipped her onto the couch and covered her body with his.

"Rafe." She laughed. "We need to get showered and dressed for Cass and Adam's house. We need to wrap presents. We really need to make that scrumptious artichoke appetizer." Even as she protested, she snagged her leg around his.

"Hm." He grazed his knuckles over her pretty rosy cheeks. "Right now, we have different priorities."

"Oh," she said, locking her hands around his neck. "What's your priority, teasing me about our amazing, gorgeous tree?"

"Making new traditions with you."

"Oh yeah?" Her voice soft, her body relaxing under his—this was all the present he ever needed under his tree. "Like what?"

"Christmas make-out on the couch." He rested his lips on hers and watched her eyes shimmer with heat.

"Our own traditions?" she whispered, and sent his entire body come alive at her soft voice, a musical note tuned solely for him.

"Mm-hm. Soft fire, snow outside, you and me wrapped up in each other."

"I love you, Rafe Holmes."

Rafe kissed his love into Poppy, his soulmate, the sunlight brightening his world.

* * * *

"Wow, Cass, your house is fantastic," Poppy said as she twirled in the open living room and kitchen.

"Isn't it awesome?" Cass took Poppy's coat. "Wait until summer when the garden is in full bloom and we can eat outside."

"I can't wait. I-I'm... Uhm, I decided to stay here, with Rafe."

Cass' eyes grew wide. "Oh, that's awesome! Your cousins and, well, *everyone* is going to be thrilled." She enveloped Poppy in a hug and yelled, "Poppy's staying here with us in Graciella!"

Poppy glanced at Rafe, and he gave her his sexy grin, not looking the least bit upset that she'd spilled the beans on their decision. Everyone important in her life was present. Her mom and Will, her aunt and Javier, her new friends, her cousins and their wives. Turner stood in the dining room pouring champagne and wine, his grin aimed right toward Lily and their newborn. Christmas evening appetizers with family was one more tradition Poppy could carve into her memories.

Gabby rushed over to give her a hug too. "I'm so happy you're staying, Poppy. It never felt right when you left."

Miranda gathered with them. "Please tell me you're going to do something amazing with your sewing. I could use a pretty new blouse or dress that doesn't require me going to Portland or Seattle to shop."

"I did mention your house in town has possibilities." Her mom was there, by her side, with Will behind her. They both wore genuine smiles on their faces.

"I'm sorry I didn't tell you yet. We, Rafe and, I just talked through everything last night." Cass tugged the ladies away, leaving Poppy with Anne and Will. Gosh, her mind was mush. No, not mush—flowing with emotions and love and dreams, with peace and connection and excitement all at the same time.

"Honey." Her mom wrapped Poppy in her warm arms. Mom hugs were the best ever. "I knew the moment I saw you with Rafe that you two had found something special. It's not every day we meet our soulmate and get to build a life with them. Good for you for grabbing hold. The house is a great bonus to create fabulous dreams."

"Thank you so much," she whispered against her mom's cheek. "Will." Poppy pulled away from her mom and faced her stepdad. "I'm so sorry you went out of your way to help me with Paris."

"Nope," Will held up his hand. "Stop right there. It's obvious to me how happy you are. You belong here, kiddo."

Will tugged her into his arms and Poppy smiled at the happy tears gracing her cheeks. Will's words and the fact that even he could see it meant so much to her. *Belonging.* It had been her wish for so long. And for so long she'd buried it under work, under achievement, under other's expectations, and worst of all, under fear. Carving all that away had left her vulnerable and truly able to love and be loved. "Thank you so much," she said.

When she stepped back, Rafe was there, by her side. He tucked her hand in his and gave it a squeeze. "Okay?"

Poppy nodded and gave his cheek a kiss. "I'm awesome."

"Everyone have a glass?" Adam asked. He and his brothers passed around drinks.

"To family, old and new," Cruz said and raised his glass.

"To family!" Everyone said and clinked glasses.

Rafe wrapped his arm around Poppy and touched his glass to hers. "To family. To love."

Oh, her heart melted right there into a million pieces. She was the luckiest person on the planet. She did belong here with these people, her family. And in the arms of her true love.

After the toast, Cass put on music, and they ate and drank and danced and laughed themselves silly on a snowy Christmas evening.

* * * *

"I've never been so tired and so happy at the same time," Poppy said quietly as they climbed the stairs to go to bed, late that night.

"Mm." Rafe had his hands on her hips as he followed her. She was tired and he didn't want her to fall, but he also loved touching her. Plus he wanted to be close to her when they made it to his bedroom. *To our bedroom.* That thought brought another smile to his face. He hadn't smiled this much in his life.

"Rafe..." she whispered in awe.

God, he loved how she didn't hide one single emotion. She let them all hang out. And he soaked them up, like he'd been starving for them, because he had been. Empty and alone and starving for love, for affection, for her.

"What do you think?" He'd bought more white Christmas lights than they'd needed and hung them in their bedroom this afternoon right before they'd left for Adam and Cass' so when they came home tonight, she'd be surprised by them. All the other lights were off. But the room sparkled and glowed. Their own night sky full of stars above them. She deserved to be surrounded by stars.

"I love them." Poppy twirled slowly around the room and jumped into his arms.

Rafe laughed as he caught her, then gentled them down to the bed.

"It's the most beautiful surprise anyone's ever given me, Rafe. It sparkles," she said in awe. "I can feel it in my heart, shimmering and gorgeous. You did that for me." Poppy snuggled against him and kissed him. "You made me shimmer with your beauty and love."

Rafe blushed. She thought he was beautiful. She thought he brought the love, but it was her sorcery that made him feel alive.

"You're right—this is the best Christmas ever!" Poppy's voice was a hushed whisper over his skin, across his cheeks and down to his neck. She put her hand on his heart and automatically he grasped it and held it to his body. "Time for another tradition." Poppy kissed his neck and started unbuttoning his shirt.

"Yeah," he ground out because he was hard already at her touch, as her fingers had his blood thundering through his body.

"Making love under sparkly lights on Christmas."

"Mm-hm." He dragged his hands under her dress, feeling the silk of her tights against her ass. "I lo-love the way you think."

Epilogue

One year later

Puffy white clouds floated against the blue sky as Rafe parked his truck in front of Poppy's shop. Behind those clouds hovered heavy gray ones. Bracing cold air met him as he stepped out of his truck. Storm was coming. Rafe smiled. Poppy had been obsessively checking the weather report for weeks, hoping they'd have a white Christmas like last year. So far, they hadn't had one flake. But it was Christmas Eve and that meant special things happened.

They'd worked on Poppy's house all last winter and spring, giving it the renovation and upgrades it needed to turn it into her shop, Pampered & Pretty. Her opening in summer had been a big hit and she'd been busy and radiant ever since. He loved seeing her flourish. She grew prettier every day to him with each challenge she faced.

New and vintage women's clothing and accessories and a few of her own amazing designs filled the space. With her mom's help, she'd turned it into a plush, gorgeous oasis, welcoming and intriguing. It had her feminine style all over it with a dash of 'pampered and pretty' as she said, because women deserved to be pampered and feel pretty.

"I'm upstairs, Rafe," she called as he entered. "I finished the last ornament."

The loft was her creative space where they'd put the table and cabinet he'd made for her. He'd built a matching set for her sewing room in their house, but she often still created in the nook, with her feet tucked under her, daydreaming in the sunlight that flowed in through the windows.

She was bent over her desk, her curls held in a low loose ponytail at her neck, pieces drifting out of the tie and over her shoulder. Sketches crowded the white walls. Different colored fabrics were draped here and there. The cozy pink velvet chair he'd gotten her was covered with patterns. It was perfectly her, a mess of her artistic talent exploding over every surface. But it all paled in comparison to her.

"Hi," she said, meeting his gaze.

He sent his gaze over her figure in a short emerald-green dress tied at the waist with a black scarf. Lacy black tights graced her legs, and she'd worn her tall, high-heeled black boots. Luscious and sexy and charming and cute all wrapped up in one package.

Mine, his heart still thundered at the sight of her. Those boots and tights made his blood thrum in need.

"Rafe?" She cocked her head, studying him.

"It's Christmas Eve." He stalked her, tried to calm his breathing as her eyes heated and sparked and her cheeks flushed. "Time for another tradition." She dropped her pen and wrapped her arms around his neck. Rafe hiked her up on her desk and ran his hands under her dress, caressing the silky softness of her tights until he reached her —

"What...?" He lifted her dress to find her pantyless. The tops of her tights stopped mid-thigh and from there on up, she was naked.

"Surprise," she whispered the word over his ear, running her hands down his spine, tugging his shirt out and grazing her fingers across his bare skin.

"Christ, gorgeous, I-I..."

Poppy brushed her lips against his, always patient with his words.

Screw words. Rafe devoured her mouth, her moans, letting her scent stir him higher. He gently pushed her back onto her desk and knelt in front of her, carefully dragging her dress up, so she was bared to him. He placed needy kisses on her belly, in between her thighs, sucking in his breath as she writhed closer to him. Finally, he placed his lips on her pussy and worshipped her with his tongue.

"I...I..." Her body shook when he sucked her clit into his mouth. "I had no idea this was a tradition." Rafe teased her with his tongue. "Oh! Again," she begged, and he indulged her.

She was so fucking beautiful when she let him see her, *all* of her. The soft, hazy look she gave him, the moans and the way she curled her body toward his mouth, begging for more. She was close and he wanted to give her this, but he was selfish now and he wanted to be inside her when she came. His craving was a pulsing beast inside him.

When he moved over her and worked himself out of his jeans to rub his cock along her seam, she sucked in a breath. And that was when he drove inside her, holding her as her entire body tightened. He dragged himself out and pushed back in, quickening his pace as he raced to the finish.

"Rafe, I can't," she screamed right before she came, shuddering around him.

"Hold on," he said, fucking her fast and hard. She was still pulsing around him, coming down from her orgasm, slick and hot. Rafe wrapped his arms around her, tugged their bodies tight together and drove up again and again.

"So good, Rafe. I can't..." Poppy clung to him, shaking her head and kissing his body.

"You can," he said. "Again. Once more, love. Lose yourself..." He drove in again. This was all speed, about chasing the storm, finding the lighting and sending both of them spiraling into the sky.

"It's too much. It's not enough. Oh God!" Poppy tensed and exploded around him in intense little bursts, and he cried out her name and followed her over.

The quiet surrounded them, save for their deep breaths as they returned to Earth. Rafe ran his hand down her arms, soothing her as much as himself.

"So many traditions for us to make with each other," she whispered, placing a kiss on his chest.

Yes, a lifetime's worth.

* * * *

Rafe wrapped his arms around Poppy as they pushed the cart through the new specialty market.

Spectacular had opened the same week as her shop had in the summer. It was a small grocery store that also had an amazing selection of wines, flowers and meals to go. Rafe grabbed bourbon and a case of wine and set them in the cart, along with two bottles of champagne. Poppy sighed in contentment when he wrapped around her again and they made their way to the checkout.

They had a turkey breast to roast for dinner, lots of herbs, butter, chicken stock, potatoes, brussels sprouts, garlic and some divine loaves of bread that were still warm as they had just come out of the oven. She grabbed two, one for dinner tonight and one for leftover turkey sandwiches. She reached into one of the bags and tore a piece of bread off, to snack on.

Rafe chuckled behind her. "Hungry?" His words fluttered against her ear and made her blush.

"Mm, starving. All that exercise." She wiggled against him. "Are you making your cinnamon rolls tomorrow morning?"

"Yep. Already have the stuff."

Rafe's homemade cinnamon rolls were another favorite of hers. In the deli, they grabbed olives and pâté, a yummy orange fig jam and a selection of salamis, plus Poppy's favorite triple cream brie for the charcuterie platter they were taking to the family Christmas get-together tomorrow. This year it was at Lily and Turner's. Poppy's mom and Will, who'd returned for Christmas this year too, were making dessert for tonight, a flourless chocolate cake Poppy had been craving for days. At the last minute, she remembered raspberries and heavy cream for her mom.

"I think that's everything," she said, glancing up at him and nearly losing her footing at the adoration on his face. He gave her that sexy grin of his and nodded, and she melted, again. How in the entire world had she gotten so lucky?

* * * *

"Rafe?" Poppy huffed out a laugh. *What in the world is he doing on Christmas morning that he had to get out of bed first?* Over the past year, she'd woken more often with him than without, and she much preferred the with. The fire in the bedroom was going and the little white lights were on. It was such a wonderful intimate place he always created for her. They'd hung a beautiful piece of landscape art over their bed, and in the summer, Poppy put vases of flowers all over the house, including in their bedroom. She and Rafe had nearly filled the gorgeous bookshelves he'd built downstairs. And she'd framed one of his intricate irrigation drawings and placed it near the nook. Their house had become a home.

Now where was he? She pulled the sheet up with her and fingered the curtain open. *Oh, loveliness!* Snow blanketed the land and was still falling in fast enormous flakes. Their very own winter wonderland. Something caught her eye. Resting on Rafe's pillow was a black velvet box on a pale green note. Poppy gasped, her gaze flying to the doorway where Rafe leaned against the frame, piercing her with those gorgeous dark eyes of his.

Slowly she hugged the box and note to her chest. "Rafe." Her throat was already choked up. "Come here." Never taking his eyes from hers, he sat on the bed, gently took the box from her hands and kissed her.

"I-I had to write it, so…" Rafe let out a ragged breath. "Nerves."

Poppy kissed him again. Her nervous, amazing, wonderful love. "I love your notes. They are so precious to me."

He already knew this. For her birthday in the summer, he'd made her a beautiful box to keep her notes in. She'd placed it in the drawer of her bedside table. Most of the notes were there, excluding several she'd tucked around the house because she loved them so much. She even had a few at work on her idea board.

She fumbled with the pretty green paper with a lacy cutout edge, brushing away a tear in the process.

Poppy, my love,

Oh Lord, the waterworks started with one phrase. He knew how to treat her heart with such grace and care.

You blew my world open last year when you arrived. You brought the sun and with it the warmth. You brought delight and fun and laughter, now so necessary to my life. You brought passion, desire and love, and turned my world into a dream I never felt worthy of imagining. The beauty in your heart and in your smile stuns me every day. I don't want to write too much, because I need to save some words for the notes I plan I writing you during our life together, if you'll have me. Marry me, Poppy O'Brien. I love you. Your Rafe.

When she faced him, he had the ring box open. Inside was a gorgeous pale green oval stone set in an intricate vintage gold band with a sprinkling of tiny almost black diamonds curving off to one side.

"Rafe," she whispered. "It's the most beautiful thing ever."

He shook his head. "You are." He took the ring from the box. "Peridot, matches your eyes. They-they say it comes from the sun, like you. Marry me? Let me love you?"

"Yes!" She nodded at the same time as he slid the ring on her finger. "I love you so much, Rafe. If I'm the sun, then you are all the stars in my midnight sky. You love me despite my messes and my wacky emotions and food cravings."

"No." Rafe placed a finger against her lips and pulled her onto his lap. "I love you *because* of all of that."

Poppy wrapped her arms around him and tugged him flush against her so she could feel their hearts beating together. Their hearts *always* beating together. "Best Christmas ever!"

"Yeah," he agreed before he tugged the sheet off her body and worshipped her.

* * * *

They were the last ones to arrive at Lily and Turner's house, and the place was buzzing with people and music and joy. Poppy handed out the gifts she'd made for each family. Handmade stuffed fabric ornaments, each one with a black-and-white photo printed out on fabric as the center of each ornament. Then she'd decorated them with ribbons and sequins, so that the picture was framed beautifully. Inspired by nostalgia and the old box of photos she and her aunt had been looking through last week, she'd made them with a vintage feel. Now all of them had a picture of their family to hang on their trees tonight.

"Oh, Poppy," her aunt whispered. "It's lovely. What a beautiful idea. I've never seen anything like it. And where did you get this picture?"

"I took it at Cass and Adam's wedding," Miranda said. "You and Javier were beautiful holding hands in the doorway with the sparkly lights around you, highlighting your love. I tried to use a picture that showed love for each of you. And I had so much fun making them."

"Wow," Lily said. She hugged Turner. "Look at us, how in love we are."

"Yeah," Turner said, gazing at Lily. "Gets stronger every day, doesn't it?"

Lily nodded and snuggled into Turner's chest.

"They are absolute treasures," Miranda said, wiping away a tear. The photo was of her and Cruz holding their kids, grinning at each other. Lily had taken that one.

"Where's your ornament?" Lily asked. "We want to see all of them."

Poppy smiled at Rafe, who had his arms wrapped around her from behind. "Well, I was hoping you all could take a new picture of us today."

Rafe twined their fingers together and held their joined hands up for everyone to see.

"What?" Lily squealed.

"Oh, congratulations!" Miranda fingered Poppy's ring. "It's so beautiful!"

"Rafe and Poppy are engaged!" Lily yelled. "Oh, it's the best Christmas ever."

Poppy nodded and laughed. She couldn't agree more.

"Well," Cruz said and aimed his camera. "Smile. You're in a perfect spot for a photo with the lights twinkling around you and the tree in the background."

And as Poppy and Rafe beamed at each other, Cruz snapped the picture.

We are in the perfect spot, right here in this house with these people, surrounded by love.

Last year she'd returned to Graciella in search of her father, in search of belonging, to understand the past and why she felt so disconnected from people. Hugging Rafe's arms around her, she grinned at the room full of family before her.

Her journey had turned into so much more than she'd ever expected. True love and yes, *belonging*, her own genuine homecoming.

One she and these people had made together.

Rescue Me: Salvaging Love
Sara Ohlin

Excerpt

Ellie was a soggy, soapy mess of bubbles and puppy fur. By some miracle, a few strands of her hair had survived the battle to bathe Chewie, one of the litter of four she'd found at the front door of her clinic, dirty, scrawny and huddled together in a cardboard box.

It wasn't the first time since she'd opened her vet clinic four years ago that animals had been abandoned at the door. Once, she'd even found a lovebird waiting for her. One lovebird. Everyone knew lovebirds were a pair. Ellie couldn't stand to see animals abandoned or put down, not if there was the slimmest chance someone could love them and give them a home.

Fortunately, these four babies would be adopted soon. Puppies always were. They were part Lab and part a whole bunch of mutt. Chewie was chocolate brown, like his namesake, and his hair was velvety and curly, more retriever-like. His shimmery brown baby eyes filled with longing every time he gazed at her. *I might have to keep this one.* As she poured water over him, he launched himself into her arms trying to cling to the large rubber apron she wore. Before she could disentangle him and put his butt back in the water, the bell over the front door rang. *Damn!* She'd meant to lock it. She kept Chewie attached to her chest with one hand, grabbed a towel to wrap around him with her other and headed out front.

Holy cow! "Can I...ah, help you?" The man stood by the front window, silhouetted by the fading evening light. Huge and gorgeous with rugged tan skin, black hair curling over his collar and the coolest blue-green eyes she'd ever seen. Ellie almost sighed, but that flash of beauty disappeared in an instant. Anger radiated from him.

"What the hell is going on, Ken?" he said into his phone, but he pierced her with his gaze.

His anger vibrated over them. Chewie started shaking in her arms and buried his head in the towel. "I'm sorry, sir, but can I help you? This is my —"

"What do I mean?" he ignored her to yell into his phone. "I'm standing here on my property that still has tenants in it. Explain!"

Sheesh. She leaned back with the force of his words. "It's okay, baby," she cooed to the shivering puppy in her arms. "Sir," she called louder this time, "we're closed right now and you're scaring the animals. If you wouldn't mind taking your phone call outside, I —"

He sliced his hand up to silence her.

Excuse me? She was not about to let this foul-mouthed jerk boss her around, but before she could say anything else, he hung up. "If you were closed, why was your door unlocked?"

"What?" It wasn't merely his size or harsh tone that had her brain malfunctioning. She couldn't keep up with his line of questioning.

"Your door," he said, his tone singeing her. "Why would a woman like you leave her door unlocked while she's here by herself?"

'*A woman like you?*' Ellie flinched. She didn't even want to know what he meant by that comment. She'd spent eighteen years of her life with people putting her down. No way in hell she was going to listen to more of it, not after she'd clawed her way out of that filth so long ago. She chose to focus on only part of what he said.

"I'm not alone." She scrubbed the soft puppy.

"Jesus." He closed his eyes.

She certainly didn't know what *that* meant. His swearing said a lot, but at the same time it didn't really say anything.

"Would you mind not swearing?"

"Excuse me?"

"I said, would you —"

"I heard you."

Okay, now she was getting angry. "Listen. I don't know who you are or what you're doing here, but, like I said, we're closed for the evening and I need to get home. You can make an appointment or come back in the morning when we open." God, she hoped he didn't come back.

"You should have been closed for good a week ago. Closed and vacated."

"What? What do you mean? This is my clinic. I signed a lease through the end of the year. That's seven months away."

"I know when the end of the year is."

The man had a degree in condescending behavior. His tone, his attitude, his entire demeanor said power and money, and the tailored gray suit, black dress shirt and shoes all bragged of wealth. The way he tried to silence her with his hand in the air. She couldn't stand people thinking they were better than everyone else. It got her hackles up. That and the way he studied her, assessing.

"I was stating the terms so you could realize your mistake and apologize for barging in here with your atrocious behavior and yelling at me."

He stared at her again. His features transformed from a pissed-off beast to a quiet, controlled predator. As if he carefully leashed his temper, and instead saw her as a problem to be solved. His eyes were calculating. It sent a nervous tingle up her spine.

"Well?" she prompted, trying to act braver than she felt. Chewie's heartbeat raced against hers. He wiggled to get loose from her tight hold.

"Terms have changed." He raised an eyebrow. Those eyes of his were a mysterious blue-green, like a deep pristine lake surrounded by mountains. And when he wasn't yelling, his voice soothed. He took a step toward her which jarred her out of her observations. She leaned back.

"What terms? Who are you?" She had to look up now. Jesus, he was well over six feet tall.

"Jackson Kincaid. I'm the new owner of this block. I'm tearing the entire thing down. Everyone was supposed to be vacated last week at the latest," he finished, delivering the blow to her gut just when the wriggling mass in her arms threw himself onto the floor and shook his sudsy, wet puppy body all over the man. Unable to find traction on the slippery floor, the pup flopped over on his back and clung to Jackson's pants with his tiny claws.

"Christ!" He reached down and plucked the pup up into the air, holding him away from his body.

"The new owner? Of the whole block? And you're tearing it all down?" She was surprised she could even find her voice at the shock. "You can't."

"I can," he said, glaring at her with that raised-eyebrow thing he did that made her feel ten instead of twenty-seven.

"Can't." She'd found her voice again, getting pissed.

"Can," he said, leaning in.

"You're a bully!" Anger heated her blood. "You don't even know me or the Heelys, or Carl and his daughter. I know your kind. And I won't let you come in here and intimidate me."

"You won't?" He looked at her questioningly. Or was he teasing her? She'd been so busy yelling, it almost sounded now as if he were fighting back laughter.

"No, I won't."

"And how do you plan to stop me?"

But she didn't get a chance to speak because Chewie let loose and peed all over Mr. Bully, drenching his perfect-fitting suit and his expensive leather dress shoes.

Ellie watched, frozen in place while he blinked. *Oh, shit!* "I...I am so sorry. He's just a, well—"

"Puppy. Got it," he clipped.

"Someone left a litter at the door and I had to get them clean. He's not trained."

"Yeah. I got that too."

"Here," she said quietly, trading him a towel for Chewie.

"Fuck! This day keeps getting better. Slime of the earth in my office earlier. Get over here to check out my buildings, find the tenants still here, an ignorant blonde and now I have puppy piss all over me." He wiped at his wet shirt and jacket with the towel.

She soothed Chewie and bristled at the *ignorant blonde* comment.

"Look, I'm sorry about what happened, but there's no need to be rude. You don't know me, which means you don't get to call me ignorant. What *I* know from *your* behavior is that you're an arrogant jerk who needs lessons in manners."

His eyes met hers, and the heat in them made her suck in her breath. Okay, maybe she'd gotten carried away and should *really* learn when to stay quiet. He acted like a jerk, but it wasn't like she had to point it out to him. Belatedly she realized it was kind of like teasing a hungry lion.

"Not ignorant?" His voice had turned low. Yup, definitely poking a lion. "You're here alone. It's dark. Every store along this street is closed. It's a sketchy neighborhood at best, and you leave your door unlocked?"

"Why do you care?" Ellie was confused by this entire conversation.

"Why?" He prowled closer. Okay, she should definitely be more careful about locking her door. "You. Here. Alone. Any cracked-up junkie could come right in and take what he wanted." He waved his hand up and down her body to indicate what that might mean.

"Now you're freaking me out *and* being rude." Her voice wasn't above a whisper, but he heard it.

"Good!"

"Good?"

"Yeah, maybe you'll be freaked out enough next time to lock your fucking door."

Okay, she was exhausted, and hurt by his words, although she didn't understand why, since he was nothing to her. She wasn't good in situations like this — no matter how many years and miles away she was from her childhood, nasty people still affected her ability to be strong. It was painful to realize she hadn't gotten better at handling it at all. "Right. I understand," she began without any of the anger or passion lacing her words. "And I, ah, appreciate your concern, even if it's delivered in a yelling, jerky way, but you don't need to worry about me."

He braced back as if she'd slapped him. "You're kidding me?"

"No. Anyway, my night vet tech should be here any minute. Plus, I have Buffy. She's a great judge of character."

"Buffy?"

Ellie pointed toward the corner where her ten-year-old, one-hundred-pound Rottweiler slept on her dog bed, snoring away.

"Right, I can see how Buffy, who hasn't moved a muscle except to snore since I got here, is a perfect guard dog."

Ellie brushed back the curls that had slipped out of her ponytail. "If we continue this conversation tonight, you're going to throw your stuck-up disbelief and insults in my face, and as pleasant as it seems to be for you, it's not for me.

"I've been here since six, on my feet all day, which normally I don't mind because I love my job, but I had a horrible surgery on a dog. My assistant left at noon. I still have to get this little guy and his siblings settled for the night, which means fed, taken out to pee, shots and crates. I haven't eaten since breakfast. Dinner is a peanut butter and jelly sandwich before I face-plant into bed. You come in and threaten my clinic, no correction, my *dream*, which I worked my butt off to open. Maybe you could come back tomorrow, or we could meet for coffee and you can tell me, if you really are the new owner, what I have to do to convince you not to tear this block of buildings down. Then we can both go our separate ways and never see each other again."

It almost hurt her to say those words, because even though he was a total jerk, he was beautiful to look at. But horrors could hide behind beautiful appearances, something she was all too aware of. After all, her mother was a gorgeous model, but underneath she was crazy mean, and Ellie was the one who had taken the brunt of it.

He studied her while she spoke, silent and assessing again. Then he reached by her to grab one of her business cards from the counter. "Dr. Ellie Blevins, you think you can convince me not to tear this bag of bones down and build up a new condo development that will make billions?"

Billions? Did every battle she fought in this life have to be so outrageously difficult? This block was special. It wasn't only her clinic. It was the bakery, the hardware store that Carl and his daughter ran, her friend Ruby's spa, Lachlan's pub. This neighborhood burst with potential. And the park at the end of the block right along the river was lovely. The bonds she'd formed here, the true friendships, would make her fight back, even if she didn't feel brave enough for herself.

"It's not a bag of bones. It's a block of old, historic buildings that need love and care," she began. But standing there, taking in his polished rich-man strength, it was futile to convince him of anything. "You know what? Deal me the death blow now. I'd like to review the lease I signed before I throw in the towel and start looking for a new space and a new home, because I can tell there's no way you and I will ever be on the same page."

"New home?"

"What?" she said.

"You said, 'a new space and a new home'?"

"I live in the apartment above the French Connection Bakery. Mr. and Mrs. Heely have owned it for twenty-five years." There she was, exhausted-sharing again. And there he stood intense-staring. She closed her eyes at the craziest, weirdest conversation she'd ever had, and realized Chewie was asleep on her chest with his tiny head nuzzled in her neck. *Oh, soft love*, she thought, *if only people were more like dogs, so trusting, kind, and loving.*

"One month," he said.

"One month to be out of —"

"I'll give you one month to try to convince me."

"I... What?"

"You spend time with me for the next month. We get to know each other, and you can state your case."

"Spend time with you?" *Is he insane?*

"You said you wanted to try to convince me to change my mind."

"Oh," she whispered, confused again.

"You open tomorrow?"

"Yes," she said quickly, thinking maybe they'd tested each other's patience enough for one evening.

"Right, then. Tomorrow. Lock your door." Then he was gone, leaving her more confused than ever.

"Lock your door!" he yelled from outside, startling her out of her spot.

She went to the door, locked it, drew the blinds down and blew out a breath. "What in the heck just happened? I feel like a tornado blew through here and tossed us sideways into outer space. And what does 'tomorrow' mean? Is he coming back? Am I supposed to appear before him like a magician?"

She looked at Chewie and spoke into the empty waiting area with Buffy chasing squirrels in her dreams. *Holy cow! Holy freaking cow! This place is everything to me, more than my hopes and dreams – it's my safe place.* One single month to convince an angry lion not to eat her up? She might be an awesome veterinarian, but there were absolutely no instructions for how to communicate with a beast like Jackson Kincaid.

About the Author

Puget Sound based writer, Sara Ohlin is a mom, wannabe photographer, obsessive reader, ridiculous foodie, and the author of the contemporary romance novels, *Handling the Rancher*, *Salvaging Love*, *Seducing the Dragonfly*, *Igniting Love* and *Flirting with Forever*.

Sara loves creating imaginary worlds with tight-knit communities in her romance novels. She credits her mother, Mary, Nora Roberts and Rosamunde Pilcher for her love of romance.

If she's not reading or writing, you will most likely find her in the kitchen creating scrumptious meals with her kids and husband, or perhaps cooking up her next love story.

She once met a person who both "didn't read books" and wasn't "that into food" and it nearly broke her heart.

Sara loves to hear from readers. You can find her contact information, website details and author profile page at https://www.totallybound.com

Home of Erotic Romance

Sign up for our newsletter and find out about all our romance book releases, eBook sales and promotions, sneak peeks and FREE romance books!